He'd Always Been A Romantic,

always liked every part of loving a woman, from the teasing to the wooing to the savoring power of pleasing a woman in passion. Until Gwen's defection, he'd never had a reason to doubt his ability to satisfy a woman. But with Regan, those needle pricks of doubt were full-scale daggers. He had to be nuts to think of falling in love with her. She was a sensuous woman, right down to her fingertips. He wouldn't have a clue how to please her.

And the thought of failing her rammed a tight feeling in his chest. She *was* vulnerable. She'd been hurt by men before. And, dammit, he wasn't going to be another in her long list of so-called heroes who'd turned out to have feet of clay....

Dear Reader,

This month we have some special treats in store for you, beginning with *Nobody's Princess*, another terrific MAN OF THE MONTH from award-winning writer Jennifer Greene. Our heroine believes she's just another run-of-the-mill kind of gal...but naturally our hero knows better. And he sets out to prove to her that he is her handsome prince...and she is his princess!

Joan Elliott Pickart's irresistible Bishop brothers are back in *Texas Glory*, the next installment of her FAMILY MEN series. And Amy Fetzer brings us her first contemporary romance, a romantic romp concerning parenthood—with a twist—in *Anybody's Dad*. Peggy Moreland's heroes are always something special, as you'll see in *A Little Texas Two-Step*, the latest in her TROUBLE IN TEXAS series.

And if you're looking for fun and frolic—and a high dose of sensuality—don't miss Patty Salier's latest, *The Honeymoon House*. If emotional and dramatic is more your cup of tea, then you'll love Kelly Jamison's *Unexpected Father*.

As always, there is something for everyone here at Silhouette Desire, where you'll find the very best contemporary romance.

Enjoy!

Lucia Macro

Senior Editor

Please address questions and book requests to:
Silhouette Reader Service
U.S.: 3010 Walden Ave., P.O. Box 1325, Buffalo, NY 14269
Canadian: P.O. Box 609, Fort Erie, Ont. L2A 5X3

JENNIFER GREENE
NOBODY'S PRINCESS

SILHOUETTE *Desire*®

Published by Silhouette Books

America's Publisher of Contemporary Romance

SILHOUETTE BOOKS

ISBN 0-373-76087-6

NOBODY'S PRINCESS

Printed in U.S.A.

JENNIFER GREENE

lives near Lake Michigan with her husband and two children. Before writing full-time, she worked as a teacher and a personnel manager. Michigan State University honored her as an "outstanding woman graduate" for her work with women on campus.

Ms. Greene has written more than fifty category romances, for which she has won numerous awards, including two RITAs from the Romance Writers of America in the Best Short Contemporary Books category, and a Career Achievement award from *Romantic Times* magazine.

One

Alex Brennan had never considered himself a hero, but he believed that a good man lived his life by certain unshakable rules. The strong had a responsibility to protect the weak. A decent man never backed down from a principle. A guy without honor was lower than pond scum.

That code of values was so ingrained that Alex rarely even thought about it. Until recently.

Two weeks ago—specifically the day his bride stood him up at the altar—Alex had accidentally started noticing that a bunch of heroes throughout history had a common problem.

Good guys had notoriously bad luck with their girls— and it was never more obvious than in the movies. Bogart, for instance, was left standing alone at the end of *Casablanca*. Gable never did get Scarlett. Costner went through all that bodyguarding nonsense with Whitney and ended up with a song instead of the girl.

Late-afternoon sunshine speckled light and shadow on the dusty bookshelves of the public library. A winsome, whispery breeze redolent with magnolias drifted through the long, tall windows. The library was as lively as a morgue—which suited Alex's mood to a *T.* No place on the planet beat Silvertree, North Carolina, on the first of May—every sane person in town had succumbed to the irresistible "spring fever" day and was out playing hookey. The deserted library offered him an ideal place to brood. He thumped a pencil end-to-end on the old, scarred oak table, as he further considered the problem.

Those old tales seemed…well, telling. Heroes might conquer dragons, build a couple of empires, save mankind from some horrendous evil. But being good guys didn't seem to guarantee success with their best girls. Maybe honor wasn't sexy. Good guys just didn't seem to stir a woman's heart the way the bad boys did. A taste of *wicked* not only seemed to appeal to the delicate female gender…but they seemed to find good guys downright boring.

A loud kerthump made Alex's head shoot up. Someone had dropped a book in one of the nearby aisles. The thump was followed by a colorful expletive in a throaty female alto. Except for the librarians at the front desk, Alex had thought he had the place to himself. But beyond being temporarily startled by the noise, he paid no attention.

Research tomes were precisely stacked in an impenetrable blockade all around him. Technically he'd popped into the library to prepare for tomorrow's class. High school kids today hated learning history as much as he had—which was why he'd broken with all Brennan tradition and done a damn fool crazy thing. He'd become a teacher.

Alex never really felt he had a choice. Someone had to make history exciting to the kids. Someone had to convince them that history was more than dry dates, but a record of drama and courage and the power of the human spirit. Unless the kids understood how the human race screwed up, the next generation was just going to repeat the same mistakes. Teaching history was about making heroes come alive and serving them up to kids in the way of role models.

Of course, a teacher had to keep the bubble gum generation awake to instill any of that. It was challenging to keep a *dog* awake on the semester covering medieval history, but Alex theorized that he could spice it up with some King Arthur lore—hence the weighty research tomes piled on the table around him. The ideals in the Arthurian legend were the stuff that lifted mankind from the Dark Ages—honor, loyalty, justice, chivalry. Camelot was meant to be a land where fairness and truth were nurtured, where beauty thrived, where love was an ideal.

But Alex had barely opened the first text before the dark, broody mood kidnapped his attention. The problem was the legendary King Arthur. He was another blasted hero who'd lost his best girl. Another good guy who hadn't done one thing wrong. But because honor couldn't compete with a younger, sexier stud named Lancelot, Arthur had lost everything.

Alex wasn't inclined to take the comparison too far. He was no King Arthur. Still, he knew that precise feeling of loss. Painfully, intimately well.

Another kerthump sounded from the next book aisle over. Then another. Followed by a trail of extremely loud and colorful curses from the same throaty female alto.

Alex shot an exasperated scowl in the general direction of Ms. Klutz. No one, but no one, ever hung out in the myths and legends section but him. And especially on this to-die-for spring day, he should have been guaranteed a private refuge in this back corner of the library. Couldn't a guy wallow in a deep, dark case of self-pity in peace and quiet?

Apparently not. He'd barely thrown down his pencil before the lady abruptly charged around the corner, juggling a good dozen hefty books and heading for him at a dead run.

For a second Alex froze like the iceberg in the *Titanic*'s path. Not that the woman was so big—the tonnage of books teetering in her arms looked bigger than she did. But she was obviously hustling to get them to the table and set them down before they all toppled and fell. The mission was doomed. Alex caught a fleeting impression of flashing scarlets and wild silky hair before disaster struck.

She made it to the oak table, but not before the volumes started shifting and spilling. Her river of books crashed into the sea of his. Several sailed to the floor; one ended on his lap.

Curses followed. Not his. Being out of breath didn't seem to limit her vocabulary, and totally incomprehensibly—once she got rid of her armload—she started laughing.

"I'm sorry, I'm sorry! You just can't imagine the day I've had. It's been one thing after another.... Here, I'll get that. You don't have to help—"

Alex instinctively sprang to his feet. Helping a lady in trouble was second nature, an integral part of the Southern gentleman's code he grew up with—but in this case, basic survival instincts were the far more powerful motivator. God knew how much more damage she could do if left to her own devices.

She was breathlessly huffing and puffing as she bounced down to pick up the fallen books. On one of her bounces back up, her elbow came mortifyingly close to a poke in his crotch. He opened his mouth, closed it faster than a fish and caught a noseful of some spicy, exotic perfume. By the time he'd rescued the last of the fallen books, she'd managed to knock over more of his meticulously neat research stack.

"I'll get it, I'll get it. Sheesh, I'm sorry—"

"Nothing to be sorry about. Accidents happen."

"All I had to do was make two trips, but no, I was trying to save time and carry all the books at one time. It's just that they were all so heavy—"

"I can see that."

"I must have sounded like a bull in a china shop, but I never expected to find anyone else back here. I've come to think of this as my sacred spot because no one else is ever back here. My air conditioner at home went on the fritz, and I just needed to get in a couple hours' work where it was cool—you don't mind if I sit at the same table, do you?"

Mind? Alex craved peace. He needed quiet. The Silvertree Public Library had two stories of sprawling space for her to choose another table. And not that a gentleman would ever lift his territorial leg on a lady, but he was here first. Still, manners had been imprinted so deeply in the men in his family that his response was automatic.

"No problem," he said, and then swiftly pulled a book in front of him and ducked his head.

Eventually she quit huffing and puffing. Eventually she sat down. Eventually she noisily rearranged her hodgepodge of books and clattered in her purse for a pen, and finally—there was a God—she settled down.

Alex couldn't.

He vaguely recognized her. Typical of North Carolina small towns, Silvertree was a friendly place. Maybe they'd pulled into the same gas station, or he'd seen her in a grocery store or on the street. Alex couldn't imagine a man younger than 105 who'd fail to notice her.

She was several inches shorter than his six feet, but her figure—delicately speaking—could inspire a guy to crash a car or two to get a closer look. Her hair was caramel brown, shoulder length, with silky scoops of curls all over the place. No order. No control. Which about summed up the rest of her as well, Alex mused.

A long sun-shaped earring dangled from one ear, a long moon earring from the other. Apparently they were a matched set. She was wearing a scallop-necked red T-shirt—snug enough to give a man a heart attack—and a long skirt that was a swirl of colors: fuchsias, oranges and reds all blurred together. Her sandals showed off red-painted toenails—about the same color as her strawberry lipstick. Bracelets dangling clanged every time she moved.

Alex wasn't *trying* to sneak looks at her, but she moved a lot. And every time he glanced up, faster than bad news, he found her hazel eyes on him.

Her eyes were huge. Deep set and as lushly dramatic as the rest of her. She wasn't precisely pretty, but her oval face had a complexion as pale and soft as vanilla, with high broad cheekbones and a full sensual mouth. Her face was unignorably striking, and her figure was downright dangerous. The skirt concealed her legs, but she didn't appear to be carrying any spare pounds—except upstairs. The stretchy T-shirt made no secret of the lush, voluptuous curves above her waist.

She was…Alex searched his mind for the right descriptive term. *Sexy* shot to his brain faster than a bullet, but was swiftly, uneasily rejected. Hell, he hadn't thought of a sexist term like that since he was a teenager. *Alarming* was more like it.

In fact, *alarming* seemed to describe her perfectly. There was nothing wrong with her haunting hazel eyes, flashy style or mesmerizing red mouth. But Alex's taste in women had always been more like…well, like Gwen.

His fiancée had been petite. A lady, inside and out. Gwen was soft-spoken and soft-mannered, prone to wearing fragile feminine pastels that suited her blond-and-blue-eyed fairness. She'd been everything Alex had ever dreamed of in a woman. Everything he'd waited a lifetime to find.

Until she'd left him at the altar, and run off with a ten-years-younger, good-looking rogue named Lance.

"You look really caught up in sad thoughts."

Alex's head shot up. "Beg your pardon?"

Those huge hazel eyes were all over his face again, studying him as intrusively as a cop could frisk a suspect. "I don't mean to pry. You just had this look, as if you were carrying the weight of the world on your shoulders. Are you okay?"

No, he wasn't okay. He wasn't remotely okay. But he didn't know the woman from Adam, couldn't believe she would ask a total stranger such a nosy question. And for sure, he couldn't imagine how to answer it.

His reticence seemed to fly right by her. The undauntable woman smiled…a slow, warm smile that crinkled those eyes into pinpoints of light. Impulsively she leaned over the table and extended a hand, offering him a view down the scooped neck of her T-shirt that turned his throat desert dry.

"I'm Regan. Regan Stuart. I know I've seen your face around town somewhere—do you teach at the college?"

"No. That is, I'm a teacher—but I teach high school history, nothing at the college level—"

"Well, I'm a teacher, too. I thought I might have seen you around the Whitaker College library before—I'm an assistant prof, teach women's studies. And you're—?"

"Alex Brennan." He didn't want to give up his name, any more than he wanted to shake her hand, but there seemed no way of avoiding either without being rude. Her palm clapped against his in an exuberant, pumping handshake, as forthright and blunt as she was. Her skin was soft, though, and warmer than sunlight.

She dropped her hand quickly enough, but his pulse was suddenly skidding down a slick, unfamiliar road. At thirty-four, Alex was more than familiar with hormones, but it was one thing to recognize her attractiveness, and another to feel a kindling responsiveness to her. He loved Gwen. And Gwen had always inspired loving, sensual feelings in him, but not this strange, flash-fire kind of sexual awareness.

It made him feel guilty. And nervous. Quickly he stuffed his hands in his pockets and hoped she didn't notice his sudden awkwardness.

She didn't seem to. Nothing seemed to quell her gregarious friendliness. "Well, nice to meet you, Alex. It's really rare I find anyone in the myths and legends section but me, and I couldn't help but notice all your books.... You're preparing for a class?"

"Yes. And I'm afraid I really have a lot to do." Thankfully, she took the hint. Her head ducked, then his head ducked. Pages turned. A spring-laden breeze whispered in the open windows. It was peaceful just like that.

For maybe two minutes.

"Do you like teaching?"

Hell. It was like trying to concentrate with a fire alarm going off next to him. He wasn't sure why she kept ringing his personal fire alarm, but she was far too disturbing a woman to possibly ignore.

"Yeah, I love teaching," he answered her, and heard the instinctive stubborn note in his voice. He got grief all the time—especially from his brother, Merle—on his choice of career. The Brennans were one of the old, landed families in Silvertree. Few in the community could fathom what the Sam Hill he was doing in a classroom. Alex didn't care what anyone thought, but he was used to no one understanding.

"Me, too. I *love* working with young people. I even believe that corny line from the Whitney Houston song about 'the children are our future.' Can't imagine doing anything else." All animated, she leaned forward, giving him another throat-parching view. "You've really got me curious, though. I see all the books around you on Camelot and the Arthurian legend...but I thought you said you taught history?"

"I do. But we're in the medieval stretch. The kids are in no big hustle to get excited about 1066 and the Battle of Hastings."

"I'm with them." Her eyes danced with teasing humor. "I can well imagine that King Arthur is an easier sell."

"*Anything's* an easier sell than the Dark Ages. And it's not like I can't teach them something from the Camelot legend. Half our political concepts about equality and democracy came from the ideals emerging in that time...." Alex suddenly frowned, startled to realize he was actually inviting more conversation with her.

She seemed at ease, as if they were old friends. "Yeah, I practically inhaled the Camelot story when I was a kid. I'm no believer in heroes, but Arthur seemed to be one of the true-blue good guys. It's just a shame he was so brain smart and so life dumb."

"Life dumb?"

"Uh-huh. All those brilliant ideas and ideals, but he didn't seem to have a dog's sense about people. I mean, look who he picked for his pals. He trusted Lancelot— who wooed away his wife right under his nose. And he fell for Guinevere—who had to be one of the shallowest nitwits of all times. All it took to impress her was a young guy in a pair of tights with a big sword. If she'd had a brain, she'd have recognized that Arthur was by far the better man."

Temporarily, women taking off with other men was an extremely sore spot with Alex. So was the size of the other guy's sword. He had no desire to pick that emotional scab around a stranger, but somehow he'd gotten embroiled in this conversation and he couldn't just drop it now. "I think you may have misunderstood Arthur. There was nothing wrong with his judgment. He simply recognized that no one can help who they fall in love with. And he never blamed either Lancelot or Guinevere for being true to their feelings."

"Sheesh. Don't tell me you really believe all that poppycock?"

"Poppycock?"

He caught a dazzling sparkle of white teeth when she grinned again. Those dangerous hazel eyes of hers were still studying him. Alex couldn't imagine why. Nothing in his mirror reflected anything unusual—he was an or-

dinary six feet, blue eyes, brown hair, and he wore a
beard because he was too absentminded to remember to
shave. Truth to tell, he tended to forget his looks altogether, but he really doubted there was anything in his
appearance to attract a strikingly sensual woman like Regan.

At the moment Alex doubted his ability to attract a
stone.

Yet she was leaning forward again, as if nothing on
the planet interested her but talking with him. "Well, I've
never taught King Arthur, but you're not the only one
teaching myths and legends. I'm teaching three courses
this term on fairy tales."

"Fairy tales," he echoed.

"Fairy tales at the adult level. For women. In other
words, all the poppycock lies we've sold ourselves
through history…knights in shining armor, happily-ever-
afters, heroes—all that humorous boloney."

"You think heroes are *boloney?*"

"Did I, um, touch a nerve?"

Of course she didn't. He didn't even know her. He just
felt compelled to tactfully correct the drastic misconception in her thinking. "You don't believe in heroic behavior? That a critical part of the teaching job is to instill
ideals and role models in young people?"

"Well, sure. But I also believe young women have
been brought up for centuries, hoping to be dazzled by a
knight in shining armor, and there is no such beast. Guinevere was a perfect example. Maybe Lancelot looked
good in a pair of tights, but he betrayed his best friend
and poached another guy's woman besides. She suckered
into a classic jerk parading as a hero. She'd have been
better off understanding that there was no such
animal…you're looking much better."

"Of all the one-sided, twisted interpretations of—um, excuse me?" Her last comment had seemed to come out of nowhere.

She cupped her chin in her palm, a thoughtful expression on her face. "You really are looking better," she observed. "Color shooting up your neck. Life flashing in your eyes. You looked like you'd lost your best friend when I first sat down."

"I did."

"A love affair gone wrong?"

"As wrong as you can get. She didn't show up at the altar, and I..." Alex's voice died. Frustration clawed through him. She had everything so confused about the Arthurian legend that he'd gotten all riled up and just hadn't been thinking. He couldn't believe he'd mentioned anything about his ex-fiancée. A man took his blows on the chin. Until that instant, he'd cut off anyone who'd tried direct conversation or sympathy with him about Gwen. Something about Regan was mangling his mind.

And the terrifying woman suddenly reached her hand across the table to squeeze his. "Aw, hell, I was afraid it was something like that. What a painful thing to go through. I'm really sorry."

A librarian wheeled a squeaky cart of books down a nearby aisle. A pair of teenagers jostled each other as they walked past. The magnolia-scented sunlight was still coming through the windows...nothing was new, nothing different. Except for his sudden disturbingly intimate awareness of Regan that made no sense at all.

She couldn't possibly care about a man she didn't know, yet he had the craziest feeling she understood. The warm empathy in her eyes radiated sincerity. He wasn't expecting an emotional connection—not to her, not to anyone. And seeping through his nerves was the slow, alluring electric current flowing between her hand and his. For the second time he withdrew his hand and slammed the misbehaving appendage back in his pocket. "We were arguing," he said awkwardly, swiftly.

Another one of those slow, mischievous smiles. "Yeah. I don't believe in heroes. You clearly do. And I do love a good fight—especially on this subject—but I don't usually pick an argument with total strangers. Even on Tuesdays."

"Just the other six days of the week?"

She chuckled. "Only on days when I sense someone else likes a good, rousing debate. But besides that, you just looked like you could use a little distraction. Sometimes it helps to talk with an outsider, you know? It's not like I know you. What's the harm?"

That was the whole problem. There seemed no harm. She was unlike anyone in his life—or anyone who was likely to be—and she kept looking at him with those deep, soft eyes. And out it came. The whole corny story of a man who'd waited to marry, unwilling to settle for less than a soul mate, someone who seemed as compatible with him as two sides of the same coin. When he'd found her, his whole world seemed right. For the same reason, once she took off, his whole life seemed wrong. He couldn't shake the feelings of loss. Nothing he'd ever believed in seemed sure anymore. He had never guessed she was unhappy. He couldn't grasp how he'd failed her.

Regan listened. He didn't know for how long. Every time he quit talking, she'd ask him another question in that whiskey-smooth alto of hers. Maybe her voice had him mesmerized. Hell, maybe she did. But she didn't let up on those soft-voiced, nosy, prying questions until he was spent.

For a few moments after that, silence fell between

them. Alex was suddenly aware the bright, afternoon sunshine had faded to the hushed stillness of twilight. He felt as if he was awakening from some fruitcake spell, where he'd been someone else for a few minutes—positively not himself, because Alex Brennan never spilled his private life in front of anyone.

Then, suddenly, it was over. Regan glanced at her bangle watch and yelped in surprise. She shot to her feet. "Good grief, I didn't realize the time. I have to go!"

She grabbed her unwieldy purse and three books, then darted over to his side of the table, tilted her head and kissed him. If Alex could have guessed the kiss was coming, he might have flown for Tahiti. Or stopped her before it could happen. Or swung her into his lap and responded like a wild man who'd lost all his marbles.

He never had time to make any of those choices. The kiss was over almost before it began. He barely caught the sensation of her sun-warm mouth and the tease of a sweet, forbidden taste before she sprang upright again. She jogged back to the other side of the table, scooped up the rest of her research texts, dropped one, cursed, noisily scraped the chair...and then charged out of his life as fast as she'd charged in.

Alex sat immobile for several more minutes. His heart was slamming, his palms damp, his pulse skittery. The last time he remembered suffering the symptoms of shock, one of those female hurricanes had been terrorizing the North Carolina coast.

The hurricanes had been real. Alex wasn't absolutely positive that Regan Stuart was.

There seemed some telling evidence that she was an illusion. He'd always been comfortable around women. Quiet women. Quiet, restful, peaceful women. Regan was as blunt, bold and sexy as a man's definition of *dynamite*.

No one he could conceivably have opened up to about his life. No one who could possibly have kissed him.

Spring fever addled men's minds. Alex hadn't slept well in weeks now. Losing Gwen had dominated his mind, the wound raw and unhealable, and he figured he wasn't going to recover until he understood why she left him, jettisoned the self-pity and faced up to how he'd failed her.

Under those conditions, maybe any man could daydream up the magic of a witchy, wild Lorelei.

Alex shook his head and slowly started to neatly, efficiently gather up his research tomes. He could halfway buy the illusion thing. He wasn't himself. He wasn't thinking clearly. But Regan had definitely been real—and the proof of that was the one element in their encounter that nagged at Alex's mind like a beesting. It had nothing to do with her intimidatingly earthy sensuality or her looks or anything like that. Alex couldn't imagine a man alive who'd fail to notice those things—even if he were in love with another woman.

But Regan was a woman who didn't believe in heroes.

From the time Gwen left him, Alex had felt as if he'd lost half his soul. Now, though, he couldn't help but wonder how Regan had lost half of hers.

She hadn't said one thing about herself...and as Alex exited the library and headed for home, he doubted that he'd ever find out the answer. In a town as small as Silvertree, it wasn't that unlikely that he'd run into her. But a repeat of that strange, impossible, unsettling encounter couldn't possibly happen again.

Two

Hot damn. Regan watched the ticker tape on CNBC roll past. Her Disney stock was up a quarter point. She hit the Off button on the remote control and sat back to bask.

Teaching was her life's work, but Regan theorized that no woman could stay sane without some vices. She'd been wildly gambling in the stock market for six months now. Well...perhaps *wildly* was a slight exaggeration. Considering that her entire stock portfolio consisted of five shares of stock, Bill Gates didn't need to worry about competition from her quite yet.

"But our time is coming, Scarlett. I'm getting into this business tycoon stuff. And at the rate we're going, I fig-ure we'll be millionaires by the twenty-third century— maybe even a couple weeks sooner." The black-and-white angora cat who'd just leapt onto her lap seemed unimpressed with this psychic forecast. She nuzzled in-sistently against Regan's chin, shedding tufts of fur in every direction. "What? You want a cat treat? Don't tell me your food dish is empty again. It just can't be."

At the mention of food, Scarlett O'Haira bolted off her lap and aimed in the direction of the kitchen. Regan followed, considering that the cat, like her namesake, was pretty but dumb. She invariably fell for the wrong men without ever considering the consequences.

Regan couldn't scold. She'd once suffered the same problem.

Dusk was just falling, making the teal-and-cream kitchen shadowy and gloomy. Still, she refrained from turning on the light and carefully tiptoed across the room as soundlessly as Scarlett. The newest litter of kittens was snoozing in a pillow-lined box in the corner. None of them had a good-looking daddy—and for damn sure, they wouldn't stay sleeping long.

"You're getting fixed as soon as you wean these," Regan whispered to Scarlett, who'd heard the warning before and was more interested in gourmet food and cat treats. Silent as a ghost, Regan crouched down and lifted the ten-pound sack of cat food to the counter.

One kitten stirred. The two adult females froze in unison. Both knew there would be no peace once the hellions woke up. And then the telephone jangled, obliterating all hope. The noise made four pairs of kitten eyes pop open—every one of them full of the devil and instantly looking for trouble. Regan grabbed the wall receiver before the second ring, but already knew it was too late. "Hello—"

"Regan? This is Alex Brennan."

She dropped the cat food bag with a thump on the counter.

"Are you there?"

"Yes, I'm here—"

"Did I catch you at a bad time?"

"No, not at all...I'd just finished correcting papers and was relaxing for the evening." So to speak. One orange fuzzball had already pounced on her bare foot with razor claws. Regan hiked up onto the counter and drew up her legs. Scarlett was simply going to have to take care of her wayward children on her own for a bit.

Three days had passed since she'd met Alex in the library. He'd been on her mind, but she'd positively never expected to hear his rich, dark baritone again.

"Maybe I shouldn't have called. Don't hesitate to say if it's a problem. There's no reason you should want to hear from me—"

"I enjoyed our conversation the other day. And I'm glad to hear from you. You just took me a little by surprise—Scarlett, cut that out!"

"Scarlett?"

Regan scooped the cat off the counter, feeling more flustered by the minute. "I have a mama cat, who's trying to hide behind me rather than tend to her offspring. I don't suppose you need a kitten? Or a pair? Or, say, four of them in a package deal?"

"Uh, no."

"Now, don't rush into that no. We're talking literary legends with fur—a range of choices from Casanova to Don Juan to Henry VIII to Cleopatra. Not that you couldn't rename them, but their personalities seemed fairly obvious—two lovers, a glutton and a vamp. I'd throw in a year's supply of cat food out of the goodness of my heart—"

He chuckled. "That's quite an irresistible sales pitch—and I'm impressed with your choice of names."

"Not enough to sucker you in, though, huh?"

"Afraid not. I live with an older brother."

"He's allergic to cats?"

"No, he's just more trouble than ten pets now."

She laughed. "I have older brothers, too. Believe me, I understand. They're tougher to make behave than a pet any day."

"You're not kidding."

For a few seconds there, Regan thought her chattering was working to make him relax. But then an awkward silence fell between them, and she just wasn't sure how to fill it.

She rubbed a hand on the back of her neck, thinking of their meeting in the library—and that she never should have kissed him.

It wasn't as if she normally went around kissing strange men. And at any other time, her red-alert buttons would have been flashing special warnings around Alex.

One look at him had aroused an instant carnal lust attack. Maybe Regan was a tad cynical about legendary heroes, but that didn't mean she couldn't mightily appreciate the look of one. Images of picture-book knights on white chargers flew into her mind and clung there like glue. Never mind his contemporary Dockers and sandals, Alex had that Sean Connery look—the striking dark hair, the searing blue eyes, the proud posture and lean build. The trimmed, silvery-black beard just added to the packaging. Alex just happened to have all the equipment that revved her personal hormone engines.

At thirty-three, though, Regan was old enough to thoroughly enjoy a lust attack—and then jettison those feelings faster than bad meat. She'd once sold herself all the fairy tales about happily-ever-afters, and none of the frogs she'd kissed had ever turned into a prince. She'd successfully broken her bad habit of falling for the wrong men the easiest way—by galloping at Olympic speeds away from any guy who aroused her irresponsible hormones.

She'd have run from Alex the same way. Except that she'd seen right off that he was down in the dumps, and once she realized a broken love affair was the cause, she'd felt safe. Alex wasn't on the prowl. He seemed so hung up on his Gwen that Regan doubted he even noticed her in a personal way.

Kissing him had been a natural impulse. The story about his ex-fiancée had inevitably aroused her compassion. It was the dreadful Camelot tale all over again—a vulnerably idealistic man dumped by a damn fool numbskull of a woman who didn't appreciate a good man when she had one. Regan did. Her previous experience with frogs made her outstandingly aware of how rare good men were, and Alex's confidence had seemed so low, about life, about himself. Regan could well remember all the crippling self-doubts after she'd been shafted, and he'd just seemed to need a kiss. A gesture of compassion and support. *Something.*

Damned if she was going to regret the impulse. Possibly the texture of that warm, mobile mouth had haunted her mind, but that was like handling chicken pox. Regan was an old pro at enduring—and ignoring—her wayward fantasies. He was just a good man who'd temporarily needed someone to listen. And maybe he still did. So far she didn't have a clue why he'd called.

Neither, apparently, did Alex. He was the one to break the sudden, awkward silence by gruffly clearing his throat. "I think I should be coming up with some brilliant reason why I called. The truth is, I don't have one. I just kept remembering our conversation in the library, and I guess…well, I just wanted to thank you. I never meant to vent my problems on a stranger, and you were really kind, made me feel a lot better.''

"No problem on the venting. I think everyone needs that sometimes." Regan hesitated. If that was all he'd wanted to say, she could easily end the call. But she recalled too well those aching weeks after Ty had split for another woman. She'd felt humiliated and undesirable and painfully alone. And suddenly she twisted the phone cord around her wrist. "Besides, I really enjoyed our conversation. And it just occurred to me that we never really finished our argument about heroes."

"No, I guess we didn't—"

It wasn't the first time she'd given in to an impulse. Or even the hundredth. "Well, I'm not sure, but I think I've got a couple of steaks in the back of the freezer. You have dinner free tomorrow night? It's okay to think before answering. I should warn you there's a risk—I haven't given anyone ptomaine in weeks now, but nothing comes out of this kitchen with a guarantee."

He chuckled, but her offer had clearly startled him. "I honestly didn't call expecting an invitation—"

"I know you didn't. And I'd feel bad if you misunderstood—believe me, you made clear that your heart was still tied up with Gwen. And I'm positively not looking for anyone, Alex. I wasn't thinking 'date.' Just someone to talk with over a casual dinner."

"That sounds good, but I don't want to put you to any trouble—"

She smiled. "Throwing a couple of steaks on a grill is no trouble. Say seven?" She gave him her address. "Maybe you'd better bring boxing gloves. I have a feeling we'll be tempted to finish the fight we started the other day."

He laughed, a sound that echoed in her mind long after

Regan hung up the phone. He'd been so grave. Making him laugh and lighten up gave her a warm fuzzy from the inside out. She sat there a moment longer, her gaze wandering to the untouched mail, the dishwasher that needed emptying, then down to Scarlett, who was staring up at her with limpid eyes, surrounded by the whole brood of kittens.

"Did I actually just ask a man to dinner?" she asked Scarlett, and then shook her head and leapt down from the counter.

It would be okay. It wasn't a date. It wasn't like opening a door to some idiotic fool romance as she'd done too many times. It was just offering company to a man who seemed to need a friend. And Regan wasn't short on friends, but her natural wariness kicked in around most men. Not Alex, though. Even if he weren't still in love with his Gwen, he'd described his ex-fiancée as definitely demure and ladylike.

If his taste in women ran in that direction, she'd be safer with Alex than in a convent—because, heaven knew, she was neither.

Well, they'd either have fun, she thought, or the friendship would never develop beyond that casual dinner. Either way, she was risking nothing.

She was sure.

"You're actually going to dinner with a woman? Who is she? How'd you meet her? Where are you going?"

"Yes, I'm going to dinner with a woman. And as you might expect, she was a hooker I picked up on a street corner, led me into this red velvet den of iniquity and forcibly seduced me. Naturally, when she called and offered to lead me astray again, I immediately succumbed to temptation—"

"Very funny." Merle scowled at him from the door-way. Typically, his older brother was dressed in black jeans and bare feet and was squint-eyed from spending so many hours at the computer. "How come you didn't mention this dinner before?"

"Well, if I'd known it was going to get your liver in this much of an uproar, I probably would have. My going out to a casual dinner didn't really seem to be a world-shattering event worth mentioning." Alex emerged from the closet, buttoning a blue oxford cloth shirt. No amount of teasing seemed to lighten his brother's thundercloud frown.

"What does she look like?"

"She looks like a woman. Bumps where we don't have bumps, no hair on her chin, that sort of thing…didn't Dad give you the same lecture about the birds and the bees he gave me? Considering the extensive number of women you've paraded through here, somehow I thought you knew all this—"

Merle trailed him down the hall, as close as a blood-hound, taking the mahogany staircase two steps at a time to keep up. "You keep making jokes. But my experience with women is entirely different from yours. I suppose you think I'm coming across a little heavy-handed—"

"Try 'as intrusive as a tick.' I've never seen you pull this protective big brother routine before. To a point, it's giving me a chuckle, but give yourself a whomp upside the head, would you? It'll save me having to do it."

"I can't just say nothing—"

"Sure you can. Practice makes perfect. Give it a try."

The subtle hint flew right over his brother's head. "You've hardly been out of the house since Gwen left you, except for work. You think I don't know how badly that damn woman hurt you? And the last thing you need is another woman to put you through the wringer right now." Merle hounded him into the high-ceilinged white kitchen, where Alex picked up his wallet and car keys.

"As amazing as it may seem, I already know that. And she already knows I had a recent broken engagement. She isn't looking for anyone, either."

"They all say that," Merle informed him. "I'm telling you, you can't trust women. They're all dangerous. You can never anticipate what they're going to do. There isn't a single one who thinks like a man."

"Personally, I always thought that was the best part." Alex glanced at his watch and opened the back door. "Relax, bro. I know you care, even if you are being a royal pain. But there's nothing happening that you need to worry about. In fact, all I've done with the woman so far is fight with her."

Merle's dark eyes narrowed in alarm. "*Fight* with her? You never fight with a woman."

Alex closed the door. Enough was enough. And there was no explaining to Merle that the "fight" factor was precisely why he felt both reassured and intrigued about this dinner with Regan. His brother was right. He'd never raised his voice with a lady, much less fought with one. But Regan was simply different. Her impossibly contrary views on heroes and life guaranteed they'd find something energizing to talk about. She was absolutely like no woman he'd ever been drawn to—and for damn sure, nothing like Gwen.

He pelted down the porch steps of the wide veranda. His '47 Jaguar, gleaming black, was waiting for him in the curve of the circular drive. He had a practical enough Acura in the garage, but the antique Jag was his vice. The sports cars his brother loved had never been his style. The Jag's design was low, sleek, powerful in a quiet way, a traditional symbol of quality that lasted—it pushed all his buttons, always had.

As he climbed in, a pale wind stirred the moss in the hundred-year-old oaks lining the long drive. From the century-old gardens to the sweeping lawns to the white-pillared Brennan plantation house, the whole property was a white elephant these days—and a monster for two men to rattle around in alone.

Alex loved the history, loved the whole style of a romantic era gone by. When his parents died in a car accident, he and Merle had been seventeen and nineteen respectively—damn young—but both too stubborn to give up their home and roots or see the place sold to strangers. Neither brother expected to turn into crotchety old bachelors, much less live there forever. They'd always agreed that the first one to get married had dibs and the other would move out.

Merle, though, was pushing thirty-seven this year... and getting more eccentric all the time. He was a night owl, inventing computer games by night and handling the Brennan family fortune by day—a good thing, since Alex hadn't bothered to balance a checkbook in recent memory. God knew what women saw in him—Alex suspected he must have some appeal that eluded a brother's comprehension—but Merle had sifted through the female population in three counties. They were always bright, always lookers. And a lot of them fell under Merle's spell, but somehow the relationships didn't last.

Merle didn't believe in love—and for sure he didn't believe in the wonder of a soul mate and a lifelong committed love the way Alex did.

Or the way he used to.

Thoughts of Gwen inevitably brought heartache. Chasing those dark thoughts away, Alex grabbed the directions to Regan's from the front seat. He knew Silvertree like the back of his hand, but her house was on an unfamiliar street.

The drive led him through the Whitaker College campus, with its old brick buildings and manicured lawns. Sycamores shaded the walkways and bosomy roses climbed trellises in the traditional gardens. A few bodies were stretched out in the grass, but in the sultry heat before dusk, most students were out of sight and likely cuddled under air conditioners.

The meandering, winding campus roads were familiar, but like a surprise, Regan's street led to a section of older homes, tall Victorian types all scrunched together. When Alex parked in front of her mailbox, he climbed out and shook his head.

Hers was a Victorian structure, too, but where her neighbors had gone for standard house colors—whites, reds, grays—Regan had gone for a freshly painted teal with a mustardy-hued trim. The roof sagged in one spot. The miniature front lawn was mowed, but a wild tangle of overgrown honeysuckle and myrtle clustered around the porch. A little red Mazda, old, with a battered fender, was parked cockeyed in the drive.

The neighborhood looked like start-out houses for young couples—kids screaming as they raced through sprinklers, roller skates racketing down the sidewalks, stereos blaring from open windows. It was like another world from the shadowy, formal rooms haunted with antiques and objets d'art that Alex called home. He could feel a grin kicking up the corners of his mouth. He loved his place. But for damn sure, this was a shock of something different, an alien universe away from the heartache of Gwen and his whole normal life.

Her screen door clapped open before he'd bounded up

the first step. "So you made it! I was afraid you might
have trouble finding the address—"

"No problem."

She glanced past his shoulder. "That's quite a jalopy
you've got parked there. Now why am I not surprised
you suckered into a car with a big history? But I'll bet
the upkeep costs you the sun and the moon."

"Yeah, it does." Somehow he could have guessed Regan wouldn't be impressed by a car—or much of anything materially. His poor Jag was probably smarting at
that "jalopy" crack, but she'd already moved on.

"Well, come in, come in…although I have to say, if
you forgot your appetite, you need to go home and get
it. These steaks turned out bigger than I first thought. And
I hate to put you to work the instant you get here, but
I'm having a heck of a time with my grill—"

"I'll be damned. Don't tell me you need a hero?"

He'd almost forgotten that whiskey-wicked chuckle.
"Don't you start with me, buster. Come on in, and let
me at least get you a glass of iced tea before we start
fighting about heroes and sexist nonsense…"

Coming in was easier said than done. Kittens attacked
him the instant he walked in the door. There seemed to
be a dozen—she claimed there were only four—but all
of them were uglier than sin and old enough for trouble.
Colors splashed at him. The kitchen was a reasonably
subdued teal and cream, but then Regan hadn't likely put
in the counters and floor. Her personal stamp was everywhere else, the living room done in reds and clutter—red
couch, red chairs, books stacked and heaped everywhere,
light and heat streaming through the undraped windows.

She started talking and didn't stop. She didn't even try
to save him from the cats. "I had a roommate until a
month ago. Julie had the appalling bad judgment to fall

in love and get married, and when she and Jim moved into another Victorian place, they took the curtains from this one. I'm looking for another roommate right now. And I keep meaning to put up some more drapes, but somehow I don't seem to be getting it done. I don't seem to be getting the air conditioner fixed too fast, either, but it's cool enough on the back porch. You like your iced tea with lemon or mint?''

"Mint, if you've got it." Right now he needed the ice more than the tea. Never mind the house, never mind the cats. He was around academic people all the time, but absolutely no one like Regan.

She looked him over as if she was mentally stripping the clothes right off him…and liked what she saw. Ladies didn't look at men that way. Not in his world. And no woman, positively, had ever sent him charged messages that she found him sexually attractive and didn't mind him knowing it.

All these years, he'd empathized with women who complained about being treated like sex objects. To hell with that. This was fun. Gwen's abandoning him for a young stud scissored strips in his masculine confidence like nothing else ever had. Regan's sloe eyes checking him over boosted his ego like nothing else possibly could.

And her. Her version of casual attire was criminally short cutoffs and a flapping-loose bright print shirt. The shirt covered everything. She just wore no bra, and the silky fabric swished and cupped her full breasts every time she moved. She was always moving. Her hair had been chestnut brown the other day. Today it had a streak of blond, the style worn swept up, off her long white neck, and clipped in a pell-mell cascade. Maybe she'd brushed it. Or maybe it just always looked as if she'd just climbed out of a man's bed—after a long, sultry, acrobatic night.

There actually seemed no vanity to her. Regan just seemed totally comfortable with her body, how she looked, who she was. And that was good, Alex thought. Only his first thought—that the shock of something different was good for him—was superceded by another. His blood pressure was never going to be able to handle a whole evening. Every look at her mainlined a charge direct to his hormones. His nerves just wouldn't survive it.

She handed him a dripping glass of iced tea, and led him out to work on her misbehaving barbeque. The coven of cats followed him. She kept talking—not incessantly—but enough so he was busy answering her.

He never meant to relax. He *meant* to come up with a tactfully polite escape line and take a powder, but he had to fix her grill. By that time she'd absconded with his iced tea and returned with a tall pitcher of mint juleps. Then the steaks had to be cooked, and since he'd stayed that long...well, hell.

The neighborhood had quieted down and the sky faded to a jeweled palette by the time she served dinner on a card table on the back porch. The steaks were ogre-sized, and the baked potatoes were buried under lushly dripping butter and sour cream. The key lime pie, she claimed, was her only culinary skill, so he was ordered to save room.

Two kittens climbed on her lap, two on his. Unidentified paws kept showing up on the table, prepared to swipe any scrap—or anything that moved—and the mama cat chaperoned from a windowsill. Regan seemed to consider the cat-dominated dinner status quo. She also slipped her shoes off, and insisted he slip off his.

"This is Scarlett O'Haira's second litter. I wanted to get her fixed after the last one, but she took off with another true-love Romeo before that litter was weaned. I didn't know she could get pregs while she was still nursing, and then it was too late. I've lectured and lectured about those love 'em and leave 'em types, but when she's in love, she just doesn't listen. Have you ever seen uglier kittens?"

"Um...maybe they'll grow into their looks," Alex said tactfully.

"My God, you really are chivalrous...more key lime pie?"

"If you feed me any more, you'll have to roll me home. How long have you lived here?"

"Almost two years now. My family's from Michigan. I taught at the U of M before this. But when they started the women's studies program at Whitaker...well, the job came up right at a time when I wanted a total break. I love the warmer climate. And I thought it'd be fun to be a rabble-rousing feminist from the North on a quiet, traditional campus like this."

"And how's the rabble-rousing part of that going?"

"Not too bad. I haven't been threatened with suspension more than once a term so far." She grinned. "The girls pack my classes. That whole part's going great. But I'm allergic to those formal faculty teas. There isn't a tweed or a little flowered dress in my whole closet. And I've been known to use 'language' on occasion."

"Not that."

"What can I tell you. I was raised with four brothers. All rascals. I had to find some way to hold my own or they'd have buried me."

Maybe they were rascals, but her voice was wrapped with love when she mentioned her brothers. Alex wasn't sure where her negative views about heroes came from, but it wasn't because of them. When she lifted a plate, he automatically stood up. "I'll help with the dishes."

"Good. I hate 'em with a passion."

She wasn't kidding. She not only let him wash *and* dry, but she supervised him doing it. Alex teased her about laziness, although he had the sneaky feeling that she was deliberately giving him stuff to do to make him feel more like a friend than a guest. Probably surprising him far more than her, it was working.

In short order they'd finished the chores and aimed for the back porch again, this time settling in the rickety porch swing. All five cats climbed on laps. True darkness had fallen by then, bringing a cool breeze that sifted strands of her hair and ruffled her collar. Lights popped on in the neighborhood. Katydids called. She poured him another glass from the pitcher of mint juleps.

"Have you heard from your Gwen?"

"No."

"Do you think you will?"

The first time he'd met Regan, he thought her outspoken prying damn near close to rude. Now, it just seemed part of her, not about rudeness at all but more a gutsy honesty that was intrinsically part of her nature. And he admired it—even if she had the slight, nasty tendency to put him on the spot. "Yeah. Eventually. Gwen always lived here, and so does her family. So sooner or later, regardless of what happens with the guy she took off with, she's bound to show back up if only to see her family."

Regan reached up to unclip the hairpin, and shook her hair loose to let the breeze play with it. "That's one of the reasons I took the job here—to be able to escape having to see a guy. He taught in the same building."

Hell. If she could put him on the spot with those dicey questions, so could he. "You were in love with him?"

"Oh, yeah. Head over heels." Her eyes looked smoky by moonlight, her face soft-brushed in the silvery shadows. "His name was Ty. I could have sworn I was picking a prince. He was blond, blue-eyed, claimed to be madly in love with me right back. Until I was late one month. At which time he turned into a frog faster than a witch could wave a wand."

Late. The last time a woman had mentioned her period around him was precisely never. But she was trying to find a way to tell him, he suspected, that she'd had a "male Gwen" in her life. "He left you in the lurch?"

"I wasn't in the lurch. It turned out I wasn't pregnant. And to be honest, I admit to being careless…it just didn't seem that way at the time. We were so in love that I was positive we were headed for rings and orange blossoms and that whole shebang. I never meant to skip a pill, but when it happened I just wasn't that worried about it. Our starting a family seemed in the cards."

"It still hurts?" he asked quietly.

"Yes and no. It doesn't hurt that he's gone from my life. Once he picked up with a young female student, the handwriting on his character wall was damn obvious. But it hurts that I was so damned naive and stupid to be taken in. It's not like I was seventeen. I was too damned old to still be believing in the 'magic' of love."

He'd been keeping the swing swaying with a foot. Now he stopped. "You're serious? You really don't believe in love?"

"I believe that if two people work like dogs, they may—*may*—make a successful marriage. But I'm not sure that has anything to do with love. I think couples with stars in their eyes, looking for magic and romance,

are selling themselves lies that can seriously hurt them."
She cocked her head. "You were just burned by someone
yourself, Alex."

"Yeah. But not because either of us lied. It just didn't
work out. I wasn't the right man for her."

She shook her head vehemently. "There is no right
man. There are no heroes. Not for a man—or a woman."

Alex didn't shout at her. By the cut-and-dried code he
lived by, a man never vented temper on a woman. His
voice did sneak up another notch in volume, though, but
that was necessary. Her whole cynical view...as if love
weren't the most powerful force in the universe, as if
there were something inherently dishonest in the concept
of romance...well, he simply had to tactfully address the
errors in her thinking.

They were still fighting like cats and dogs when she
startled them both with a yawn. A quick glance at his
watch shocked him. The illuminated dial claimed it was
2:00 a.m. He shook the watch, just in case the battery
had stopped, but no.

"For Pete's sake, I'm really sorry. I know you have
classes in the morning, and so do I. I just didn't realize
how late it was getting."

He immediately stood up from the porch swing. So did
Regan, with a chuckle. "I didn't, either. In fact, it's been
a blue moon since I got so involved in a debate that I
totally forgot the time.... I'm glad you came for dinner,
Alex."

"Yeah, me, too. Thanks for the invitation." It seemed
natural to scoop up two of the kittens when she did and
cart them back to their nesting box in the kitchen. Somehow she'd made him feel at home. Alex really didn't
understand it. He'd never had a problem finding a comfort level with a woman, but this was her. Regan. Who

had his hormones in such an unfamiliar zinging uproar that he never imagined ever feeling relaxed around her.

Her house was tripping dark. Since neither of them had been inside all evening, no lights had been turned on. Just as he reached the front door, her hand reached out in the darkness to flip on the light switch in the hall. "I'll put the outside porch light on, too," she said with a chuckle. "I just still can't believe how—"

Whatever she'd been planning to say faded into cyberspace. When her hand reached out, it connected with his chest. Alex had no doubt whatsoever that the contact was accidental. His body just happened to be between her and the light switch. She was just seeing him out. Nothing had happened through the whole evening to make him think anything else was conceivably on her mind. Or his.

But there was a sudden silence in the dark hall. And her soft, warm palm froze. As if it were glued in place against his heartbeat.

Three

He couldn't be kissing her. Not Alex. Regan wasn't prone to hallucinations, but she fully respected that everyone had a bonkers moment now and then. This simply had to be one of hers. All she'd done was walk him to the door. Reach out in the pitch-black hall to flip on a light switch. And, yeah, her hand had accidentally collided with his chest. But there had been a spare second when she felt his heart beating, beating against the nest of her palm.

It wasn't as if a bomb had exploded. Or Congress had balanced the budget. Absolutely nothing monumental had happened to explain this sudden, strange break from reality she was suffering from.

So fast, so mystifyingly fast, his arms had swept around her. Regan could have handled an unwanted pass blindfolded in her sleep. But this was nothing like a pass.

The accidental physical contact acted like tinder for a spark in a dry, dry forest.

His fingers sieved and then clenched in her hair. And suddenly his mouth was just there. Covering hers. Warm. Mobile. Evocatively and distinctly male.

She swayed against him because she would have lost her balance if she hadn't. He wasn't rough. She couldn't even imagine Alex being rough. The texture of his mouth was as gentle as the disarming, winsome caress of a spring breeze...or it started out that way.

That first soft kiss deepened and darkened, scooping up momentum like the electric charge in a lightning storm. His lips sealed against hers with a pressure that made moonbeams dance under her closed eyes and the blood sluice through her veins in a giddy rush.

She wasn't going to call it magic. She knew perfectly well that physical longing and a bunch of ragtag, amoral hormones could hoodwink a woman into believing silly, irresponsible things.

But this nonmagic thing he was doing was alluring and startling and terribly unsettling. One kiss whispered into another, chained into another and another. Alex was supposed to be a gentleman. Not an inspired kisser. She'd been so positive he was on the shy side, if not downright inhibited around women, but that illusion bit the dust, too. His tongue bribed hers into trying a taste. He tasted like mint juleps and need...a raw, urgent, honest need to touch and be touched, hold and be held. He treasured her mouth, exploring, tasting, sipping her responsiveness as if he'd never sampled this gold before, as if nothing were more important in the whole paltry universe but finding her.

Images of a strong, protective knight sweeping away his lady slinked into her mind. The fantasy images appalled her. The feeling scared her far worse. She was a feminist, for Pete's sake. In her head she had no problem understanding that being swept away was unrealistic, irresponsible and outright stupid.

He loved his Gwen. She knew that, too. He was suffering from loss, and that urgent, explosive need wasn't really about her. The loneliness and longing of heartache hurt like nothing else in life. He just needed someone at that moment.

Regan played all the appropriate warning songs in her mind.

She just couldn't seem to stop her body from playing waltzes. Foolish, distracting waltzes. Her hands had somehow slipped around his waist. Her breasts crushed against his chest, her head pounding to the same wild rhythm as his, as if both of them already knew this music. His hips cradled hers, in harmony with every movement she made. He smelled like clean soap and man, pleasing, but neither scent explained this crazy feeling of drunk, dizzy intoxication.

Even as fear climbed through her system, she wanted more, not less. Even as rational thoughts tried to ground her, she didn't want to be grounded. She wanted the sizzle. She wanted the wonder. She wanted to be touched by Alex, like she couldn't remember ever wanting a man.

She could accept a moment of insanity. But something was wrong here. Really wrong. Her mind had already tabulated all the reasons why kissing him was bonkers and foolhardy, but there was something terrible going on besides that. As his tongue dove in her mouth again, as the rubbing pressure of his body speared desire through every nerve ending, she tasted risk. Threat. The power of something she was completely unfamiliar with. And it had his name.

"Regan…" She heard him groan against her mouth, saw something flash in his eyes in spite of the drowning darkness. But then he pulled back. Clenched his fingers around her shoulders as if to ensure that she was steady, and then abruptly dropped his hands and stepped away.

Regan scrabbled to recoup, not easy when she felt as shaky as a shipwreck. She could hear his breathing. And her own. Both of them were rasping as if they were mightily suffering from head colds.

Alex just stood there. He felt shock, she sensed. She understood—she'd never thought, even for a second, that he'd meant that embrace to happen. But he kept looking at her. His expression was blurred in the murky shadows, but she could see the black fire, the intensity, in his eyes.

She assumed he was suffering guilt, that all that pagan black fire must be about his Gwen. Not her. But silence stretched between them until the awkwardness was darn near paralyzing. She had to say something. "It's all right," was the best she could come up with.

"No. It isn't." Alex squeezed his eyes closed and took a long breath. She still wasn't sure what he was thinking or feeling, but Alex being Alex, his gentleman side never disappeared for long. "Regan, I seriously apologize. I'm not sure I understand what just happened, but I swear I never meant to—"

"I know you didn't. And we were having a good time, weren't we? Just being friends. We just got sidetracked for a second there. Hey, you suffered a big loss. I don't think it's any great surprise you might have needed to hold on to someone for a minute." If that was a pale interpretation of the embrace they just shared, Regan figured it was a lie they both wanted to swallow. "Don't start feeling guilty over nothing."

"It wasn't 'nothing' to take advantage of you." He

clawed a hand through his hair. "I don't know what got into me. And I wouldn't blame you for not trusting me again—"

Regan had always been better at being blunt and bossy than owning up to any vulnerability. "You didn't take advantage of me. Quit being so hard on yourself, you dimwit. We gave in to a little chemistry. It's not a hanging offense, and nothing happened that either of us need to worry about. Now go home. Get some sleep. It's two in the morning, for Pete's sake."

She kicked him out—but not before winning a startled grin out of him. Possibly no one had ever called Alex a dimwit before.

She quickly locked up and then headed for her bedroom, thinking that someone obviously should have. He'd been upset. Hell, so was she. But they'd made the mistake together, so there wasn't a reason on the planet why he should hustle in to take all the responsibility. She'd never known a man with that kind of conscience, much less one who took honor and guilt so seriously.

Until him.

Trying to distract her mind in another direction—any other direction—she flipped off the overhead light in her bedroom and started peeling off clothes. No housekeeping genie had shown up to make the bed, she noticed. The sheets and blankets were rumpled; jewelry and makeup were liberally strewn on the dresser; and the blend of startling colors would likely make Laura Ashley cringe.

Regan had long accepted that she was never going to be a shy, ladylike Laura Ashley type. She liked color. Lots of it. Heaps of it. She'd done up the bedroom with rich emeralds and satin blues with a splash of sassy yellow. Everything but the sheets came from garage sales—

no way she was sleeping on anyone else's sheets—but everything else inspired her gypsy, bargaining spirit. She resented paying full price for anything. More to the point, her taste—or lack of it—didn't have to suit anyone else. This was her haven.

Normally.

She dove for the pillows, knowing she was whipped and positive she would fall asleep instantly. Instead, she felt the cool, smooth sheet settling against her breasts and hips with an erotic awareness that had her scowling in the darkness.

Okay, so she'd been celibate for a long time. And long stretches of celibacy frustrated a woman no differently than they did a man. Intellectually, she accepted that living alone was her safest choice of life-style. Her hormones just didn't share the same enthusiasm.

The thing was, she'd always had a figure that turned male heads. She'd never asked for the overabundance of curves, any more than she'd asked for the gregarious, flamboyant personality. She couldn't help having boobs. She couldn't change her blunt, open nature.

But Regan was well aware that she'd habitually scared away the gentle guys and attracted those who assumed she was a gutsy, confident, life-of-the-party type. They weren't exactly wrong. She didn't have a demure bone in her body. But underneath, she wasn't at all carefree, and that underneath part never seemed to come out. Not with anyone, and especially not with a man.

Until tonight. Suddenly edgy with nerves, she gnawed on a thumbnail.

Nasty, terrifying feelings had sneaked up and seeped to the surface in Alex's arms. She'd never been afraid of men. She'd never been afraid of sexual feelings. Her fears were about being used and taken for a ride, because she'd fallen for Prince Charmings with feet of clay before.

But Alex was a gentle man. Not a predator. And damnation, it was downright delicious to be undone and unraveled by a lust attack for a *good man* for a change. But that was precisely the problem. Alex's integrity glowed as brightly as his vulnerability. He'd been completely honest with her about his feelings for Gwen. He needed a friend, Regan thought, and having been dumped and disillusioned herself, she even believed she could be a damn good friend to him. But to hurt a vulnerable, caring, good man stabbed her conscience with a sharp knife. Allowing hormones to enter the situation was simply out of the question.

She wasn't going to hurt him.

She wasn't going to entertain any stupid romantic notions about falling in love with him, either.

Her bedroom door creaked open, the sound so sudden and ghostly that her heart started slamming. Possibly the ghosts of past mistakes were preying on her mind. The eerie creak was followed by total silence. A frisson shivered up Regan's spine. She didn't believe in ghosts, but she had a real horror of repeating her past mistakes.

The total silence was promptly broken by a soft, telltale plop at the foot of the bed. A second later Scarlett started purring louder than thunder and sneaked up to curl in the hollow of her stomach. "Wouldn't the hellions let you sleep?" Regan murmured. "You know you're not allowed up here."

But she couldn't get into any trouble sleeping with a cat. And so she let her stay.

Alex silently opened the door to the lecture hall and tiptoed in. Only dim, dusty light filtered through the old-

fashioned casement windows. It took several seconds for
his eyes to adjust, and trying to be quietly unobtrusive,
he eased into a seat in the back row.

The wooden seat squeaked. Instantly a dozen heads
turned toward him, all female. Alex mouthed apologies
and tried to scrunch his six-foot frame into a smaller
package, feeling as conspicuous as a rooster in a hen-
house. This morning he'd determined that he needed to
see Regan, and the first chance in the day was after he
finished his own classes. But possibly he'd made a tiny
tactical error trying to catch her in a women's studies
lecture on fairy tales and myths.

The lecture hall was packed, but his beard was distinctly the only one in the place.

The hussy down at the podium shot him a wink as
soon as she spotted him. Normally Alex would interpret
that wink as a friendly, welcoming hi, but that was the
last response he was expecting. Considering what had
happened between them three nights ago, she could have
been more disposed to kick his fanny to Poughkeepsie
rather than express any pleasure at his unexpected visit.

His brother had coined the "hussy" term. Merle, of
course, had never laid eyes on Regan. He'd just leapt to
certain presumptive conclusions when Alex had walked
in around three in the morning, smelling of mint juleps
and exotic perfume.

She looked the part of a hussy, Alex mused. With only
women students in the audience, she clearly wasn't
dressed to attract a man's eye. But that splashy, dangerous sexiness of hers was like a beacon in the room. His
hormones kicked for one look at those wicked sloe eyes
and the soft, red mouth. She could undo a man with a
single smile.

He told himself he could conquer that response. He

just needed some time. It wasn't as if he'd had bomb squad training. Being around dynamite was bound to make a guy a little nervous.

She was wearing black and white today. Nothing snug, nothing tight, just a blouse in a startling geometric print with some slacks, but both fabrics were visibly soft...cupped her breasts and stroked her hips like the caress of a man's hand.

Alex shifted in his seat, trying to quell that disastrous thought train.

He was here to ask her to dinner—if and when he worked up his courage. Over breakfast that morning Merle had suggested the dinner invitation. Alex never took his brother's advice—it invariably reeked—and he strongly suspected Merle only wanted a look at her out of nosiness. But in this case he'd already intended to do it for his own reasons.

Guilt had been shadowing every step he'd taken since the evening he'd spent with Regan. He still couldn't believe he'd jumped her. He'd never failed to carefully consider a woman's feelings before laying a fingertip anywhere near her. And his mind, heart and soul—he could have sworn—were still on Gwen.

That his ex-fiancée had jumped ship on him was irrelevant. He still felt guilty and disloyal for responding so volatilely to another woman when he'd been so recently in love with someone else. And this was Regan. A woman who specifically aroused every masculine insecurity he'd ever had...and a few that were brand-new. It wasn't her fault she exuded sensuality from every pore. But Gwen's dropping him for a younger, handsomer guy had wilted any feeling of masculine prowess he'd ever had.

More to the point—at least a point of honor—Regan

had been good to him. A friend when he needed one. A compassionate, listening ear like no one else. He never should have jumped her, still didn't understand how it could possibly have happened.

It just itched on him like a mosquito bite…that he owed her. Maybe she wouldn't accept his invitation to dinner. Alex wouldn't blame her if she shot him down. But even if they were temperamentally chalk and cheese, it seemed as if they'd been developing an honest, real, special friendship—until he'd blown it. And if she'd give him another shot, he just wanted to try to make amends.

In the interim, he had a few more minutes to shore up his courage. And watching her teach struck him as a particularly brilliant way to learn more about her…although the subject matter had him restlessly scratching his chin.

"All right. Now we'll move on to 'Cinderella,'" Regan said, and thwacked a ruler in the palm of her hand. "'Cinderella' is one of the most enduring, romantic fairy tales of all times. How can you beat it? It has everything. A wicked stepmother. A pure, sweet, hardworking, vulnerable girl who's trapped in terrible circumstances. A prince in shining armor who sweeps her away and rescues her. Love triumphs. Good wins over evil."

Alex watched her spin around, her eyes flashing now.

"Consider the hidden values being sold in that fairy tale, though, ladies. We understand Cinderella is a 'good woman,' as defined by her behavior—she is meek. She is pure. She works hard, and for damn sure, she doesn't talk back. The whole plot revolves around her needing a *man* to rescue her. The fairy godmother doesn't step in to advise her on her problems, but to dress her up so she can attract this *man*. She meets this guy at a dance, gets her hormones in a dither, and she's supposed to be happy with him for the rest of her life based on a couple hours' waltzing together. Well...unless elephants fly, I don't think so.''

Several girls started chuckling. Regan hiked back up to the lectern and propped a pair of wire-rims on her nose. "Consider how long we've been selling ourselves these 'romantic' values, ladies. She's the *heroine*. We're supposed to admire her as an 'ideal woman.' But Cinderella doesn't do a darn thing in this story but be sweet and obedient and take abuse. She never lifts a finger to help herself. She certainly doesn't tell the stepmother to shove it and go out and get herself a job. She just sits there, holding out for a hero—and is totally dependent on this hero to make her life better. Does this girl need an abuse counselor or what? And how many of us were brought up believing a *man* is our answer?''

She had the girls enthralled, Alex mused. Every face in the lecture hall was focused on Regan. Nobody was chewing gum, nobody passing notes, nobody daydreaming.

Since he happened to passionately love teaching, himself, watching her in action was pure joy. Still, a thoughtful frown gradually formed on his brow. He didn't object to a word she said. None of it was an antiman type of militant feminism. If anything, she was teaching the girls self-reliance. To stand up for themselves. That there was nothing "romantic" in being weak and meek. He got it. And God knows, the girls did. Regan was funny and real and honest, and she'd charmed the students no differently than she charmed him.

Somehow, though, he heard something else under the words. Loneliness. The most painful kind of aloneness.

She didn't believe in heroes. That wasn't news. But by Alex's fundamental values, a woman should be able to depend on a man. It should be okay to be weak with someone you loved. It should be okay to turn to someone else in a time of trouble. The core of love was about that kind of trust, and Alex kept having the gnawing feeling that she didn't know it.

Disturbing, tantalizing questions prowled through his mind. *Do you really not believe in love, Regan?*

The clock behind her head showed five. With a teacher's second sense, she glanced up, caught the time and swiftly cut off her lecture with a reminder to the girls of an upcoming paper deadline.

The class was over, but a bunch of girls still swarmed her. All exuberant male bashers, as far as he could tell, hot to pursue the discussion about heroes. Regan looked up twice, trying to catch his eye, but Alex figured that a male daring to interrupt that group was risking damage to some of his favorite body parts. He stretched out his long legs, more than willing to wait.

Eventually the lecture hall quieted down. As Regan wended her way up the aisle, the last student was grabbing her books and scurrying out. The wooden door closed with a thud, leaving them alone. Regan perched on the narrow wedge of a seat. "Well, stranger. Did you come to critique my teaching techniques?"

"If I had, you'd have blown me out of the water. You're damn good, Ms. Stuart. Which is a little depressing, because I could have sworn I was pretty good in a classroom myself."

An uncharacteristic blush sneaked up her cheeks, but she ducked the compliment as quickly as the speed of sound. "I'll bet you're good. Impassioned. Dramatic. Full of fire when you're inspired." Her lips curled in a teasing grin. "What a shame you're stuck teaching a riffraff subject like heroes in history."

Her smile alone was enough to make his hormones

smoke—and so was her teasing. "Sheesh. What's it gonna take to make you believe in the good guys? We have to do something about that hard-core cynicism of yours."

"I hate to tell you this, slugger, but I call it realism."

"Yeah, I know. That's what worries me. You've obviously been disastrously misguided."

She chuckled. "I can smell a fight coming on."

If there was ever going to be a good time to slide the invitation in, Alex figured it had to be now. "I had in mind dinner first. My place. I'm afraid my brother'll hound you when you first walk in. Merle decided you must be an immoral hussy because I came home reeking of mint juleps the other night. Anything you can do to further his misconception would be enthusiastically appreciated. And in the meantime, I make a mean Peking duck."

"You're kidding. You're a gourmet cook?"

"Let's just say it'd be wise for you to fill up on the duck. The next fancy dish in my repertoire is nuked baked potatoes...but I'd like to pay you back for the other night."

"You don't need to do that." Her voice suddenly turned sober, quiet. The warning about his brother hadn't seemed to scare her, but maybe the invitation did.

"Maybe not. But we never seemed to finish our argument. I kept waiting for an opportunity to put on boxing gloves, but for some annoyingly confounding reason, we kept getting along."

"I was totally disgusted with us about that, too," she said gravely.

"So we could fix that. Get in a good down-and-dirty fight this time." Light teasing seemed to work best with her. But Alex's conscience couldn't quite leave it at that.

"And then, I'd like a chance to make up for the other night. As strong as the evidence is against me, I swear I'm capable of behaving like a gentleman."

When she cocked her chin, the pale sunlight haloed on the strong, soft line of her cheek. "I didn't notice you were guilty of anything but being human. And last I knew, that's what friends are for. Someone to be there in rough times. I tried to tell you the other night. I'm not looking for a hero. And I don't expect 'heroic' behavior."

Yeah, he knew. And somehow that was part of why he badly wanted to have dinner with her. Maybe he was recovering from a broken heart right now; but so was Regan—although she didn't seem aware of it.

Her disillusionment with heroes was something he could do something about. *As a friend*, Alex cautioned himself.

Only as a friend.

Four

Holy komoly. Alex had warned her about his brother, but the witless man had entirely failed to warn her about his home.

Regan parked her battered Mazda in the curve of the circular drive, stepped out and shook her head at the imposing plantation grounds. Maybe the history books claimed the Civil War was about cotton, slavery and states' rights, but Regan suddenly had a more brilliant insight. This was it. The real reason for the brouhaha. Someone from the land of condos and rush-hour traffic was bound to have trouble communicating with anyone who valued that whole *Gone with the Wind* life-style.

She should have guessed something was fishy when she saw his Jag, Regan mused. But it was an *old* Jag. *Really* old. Old, as in traditional, classic, historical. The kind of "boy's toy" Alex was obviously going to love.

Truthfully, she didn't have a clue what it cost, nor had she made any association between the car and money.

Still shaking her head, she started up the drive, but the double oak doors opened before she'd reached the top step of the veranda. Regan half expected the real Scarlett to flounce out the door and start flirting with the Tarlton twins, but no, it was a man framed in the doorway.

Her mouth kicked up a grin, expecting Alex—and the man was almost Alex's mirror reflection. He had the same shock of dark hair, the same searing blue eyes, the same tall, lean, broad-shouldered build. The black, collarless shirt was more contemporary than Alex's usual choice of clothing styles, but the resemblance between the men startled Regan for a second. A bemusing second. She recognized it was Merle instead of his brother for one confounded reason. Anywhere near Alex, and her heart and her hormones started doing that mortifying pit-typat thing.

His brother had damn near identical charismatic looks, and yet all she felt was curiosity. She shot out her hand. "Hello! You must be Merle?"

"Right the first time. And Alex just got stuck answering the phone—he'll be off in a minute." The handshake was over faster than a man scared of catching cooties. "Come on in."

She stepped inside and then had to blink at the sudden gloom. A dripping crystal chandelier hung over a polished parquet floor. The landing between a two-stage mahogany stairway showcased a wall of antique-framed ancestors, most of them looking forbiddingly stiff and broody. The size of the foyer could have double-dutied as an echo chamber. She loved museums, always had. She just couldn't quite imagine living in one.

"Quite a place," she murmured, and swung around to face Merle again. "I should have said who I was—"

"You didn't have to. I figured out you were Regan."

Yeah, she could feel his eyes looking her over. His assessment was swift. So was his judgment. Thankfully, Alex had clued her in that Merle was expecting a hussy— and Regan hadn't wanted to disappoint Alex. Her lipstick was Revlon Red, matching her silk blouse, which she'd worn with her snuggest white jeans, swept-up hair and a lavish dose of Shalimar.

In spite of the hall's gloomy light, she could see shrewdness and suspicion in his eyes. And liked him for it. Possibly he was normally an overbearing, nose-in-the-air jerk—how could she know? But having brothers herself, there seemed a reasonable chance Alex's brother was simply worried about him bringing home another Gwen—another woman who would hurt him. Her closet wasn't exactly overflowing with "vamp" attire, but she'd done what she could. Regan was a firm believer in dragging a problem right out in the open before it had a chance to fester.

"The living room is behind that door just off to the left. Would you like a glass of wine?" Merle asked her.

The tone was politely hospitable. The look said he wasn't going to leave her alone lest she abscond with the family silver. "A glass of wine sounds great. And I'm glad to have a couple minutes to talk with you before Alex comes in." Her voice dropped to a throaty whisper. "I'm after his money," she confided.

Merle seemed to freeze in the doorway. "I beg your pardon?"

"Well, actually, I'm after his money and his bod. I have to confess that his body inspired me first. But that was only because I had no idea he was loaded until I drove up and saw the house. Holy cow, this is a gold digger's paradise. I want you to know how impressed I am." She batted her eyelashes at him.

Possibly her eyelash-batting skills lacked a certain expertise, because something in that rigid, broody expression seemed to lighten up. He abruptly unfroze, crossed the room and poured her a glass of wine from a cut-glass decanter. "Um…why am I having this strange, psychic feeling that you're putting me on?"

"Beats me. But I'm pretty sure you must have known Alex's Gwen?"

"Yeah. Of course I did."

Regan nodded. "I've been getting the picture of Gwen as pretty close to the 'ideal woman.' A paragon of virtue. A classic lady. And somehow I suspect she fit in this house like a pea in her natural pod."

"To the manor born," Merle concurred dryly. He handed her the wineglass, but his shaggy eyebrows were arched in a quizzical expression. Possibly he couldn't quite see where these comments were leading, so Regan helped him out.

"Well, when I realized you were going to be here tonight, I thought…if you just got a look, you'd realize lickety-split that I couldn't possibly be a Gwen in training. I'm not a paragon of anything, nor aspiring in that direction. Your brother and I are just friends…. Sheesh, don't you guys ever open the drapes?"

Regan plopped down the wineglass, which she hadn't wanted, anyway, and looked around. The living room was more rampant elegance: Persian carpets, ruby-globed lamps, furniture with feet. A grand piano stood in the west corner, assuming one had binoculars to see that far. She understood the heavy velvet drapes cut out the light and heat, but there wasn't an ounce of air stirring…until she yanked open the drapes and pulled open the French doors. Fresh air immediately wafted in. Better, she thought. "Who plays the piano? You or Alex? Or is it just there to look beautiful?"

"I couldn't do 'Chopsticks' if my life depended on it. Our dad used to play, and then Alex picked it up some years ago. He's damn good, but he won't own up to it. He never plays if anyone's around."

"Hmm. Naturally the first thought that crossed my mind was that the nice, big piano top would make an ideal spot to seduce your brother. After I get him drunk and we swing from the chandeliers, of course. You *know* how wild Alex is...." She prowled the room, touching, looking. "I love old things myself, but attic and garage sales are more my speed than priceless antiques. It's a beautiful room, but where the Sam Hill do you two kick off your shoes and relax?"

Merle heaved a distinctly masculine sigh. "Regan?"

"What?"

"I'm having another one of those strange, psychic feelings. Did my brother, by any remote chance, let on that I was a little worried before meeting you?"

"Are you kidding? Alex'd take a secret to the grave. He never said a word," Regan assured him.

"Uh-huh." Laughter danced in his eyes. He didn't quite have Alex's killer smile, but it was still a charmer. "For some God unknown reason, I have the feeling we're going to get along. Although I'm hard-pressed to believe you could possibly be this full of hell around my brother."

"Oh, yeah, she can," Alex announced from the doorway. His gaze pounced on her, totally ignoring his brother. "How's my favorite hussy doing?"

"Well, I tried to talk him into a threesome, but honestly, Alex, your brother seems terribly straitlaced."

Merle clearly intended to immediately respond to this comment, but seemed to have forgotten he'd just taken a sip of wine. His response was more sputter and cough than anything coherent.

Alex still wasn't paying him any attention. "I'm really sorry I got held up. Are you hungry?"

Regan plastered a hand dramatically over her heart. "Only for you, of course."

Merle recovered in time to spit out, "You two can stop having fun at my expense anytime now."

"I was going to let Merle eat with us if he promised to behave," Alex told her. "But after that, he's leaving. He has work to do."

Several hours later, Regan couldn't help but notice that Merle had a slightly different game plan. All three of them devoured the Peking duck dinner, but when it came time for dishes, Merle remarked that maybe she'd like to see the rest of the house.

"I'm for anything that postpones dishes," she enthused, and promptly stood up, thinking that she'd have Alex to herself for a while. Instead, Merle casually tagged along with them through the mini house tour...and was still with them when they wandered into the last room at the bottom of the stairs.

It was a billiard room. The pool table sat center stage, with pecan bookcases lining the walls. The decor was Early Testosterone, Regan mused. Pipe smoke. Dust. Leather chairs big enough for the average-sized woman to nap in. Not a color or a creature comfort in sight.

"Do you play pool?" Merle asked her.

"I know one end of a cue from another, but I can't claim more than that."

"A novice, huh? But you're with friends. How about a snifter of brandy and a nice, friendly game to relax after dinner?"

She glanced at Alex for a hint if this was okay with him. It seemed to be. He hunkered down, opened a pecan cabinet, and emerged with a bottle of brandy.

Truthfully she could have used a second to recover from the house tour. The neighborhood where she'd grown up didn't have any billiard rooms. She was fond of money, heaven knew, but this level of affluence was exhausting. She'd fed Alex dinner on a card table. He'd fed her on a table big enough to skate on, and the dining room was small potatoes compared to the rest of the place.

The downstairs was common ground, but each brother had a separate, private wing upstairs. Merle's setup fascinated her. It seemed he invented computer games, and his upstairs office was a hodgepodge paradise of electronics and New Age doodads. The futuristic stuff hardly suited the historical house, but it suited Merle, who seemed to be one of a kind, with a little mysterious, eccentric side.

Alex's rooms were the ones she'd wanted to see and linger in, though, and he clearly hadn't minded showing her the house—but it was like taking a man shopping. As soon as she poked her head in one door, he was whisking her away to the next one. Still, her mind had a clear snapshot of his bedroom.

Nothing New Age for Alex. His bed was as big as Lincoln's, with a giant, intricately carved antique headboard, and pillows mounded under a sensuously plush midnight blue comforter. An intricately framed mirror offered a view of that bed—or anything that might be happening on that bed—and something in the masculine decor made her think of conquering warriors seducing maidens, or knights sweeping away their ladies under a spell of moonlight.

Impatiently Regan chose a pool cue, while Merle set up the balls and Alex poured snifters of brandy. Since she had no belief in being "swept away," damned if she could understand why the idiot thought occurred to her. He was still in love with Gwen. She *knew* that. And on her poking-and-prying discovery mission through the house, she'd seen first editions, original sculptures…but since Alex didn't seem to notice his own frayed shirt collars, she doubted he had a materialistic bone. It wasn't *things* he valued. But the ideal. The way his Gwen had been an ideal for him.

Alex carted the snifter of brandy over to her. By lamplight, his skin looked burnished bronze against his striking blue eyes. Damn the man, but she could feel his smile all the way to her toes. "You looked lost in thought for a minute there, ma'am."

"I'm awake. Just preparing to be solidly trounced playing against you two," she said with a grin. Tarnation, handling this was simple enough. She just needed to keep that "ideal" thing underlined in block letters in her head. His love for the perfect Gwen made anything but a friendship with her impossible. She took a bolstering sip of brandy. It slid down her throat like hot velvet.

Merle ambled over to the table, chalking his pool cue. "I'm thinking we need a little wager to make this more interesting."

"Think again," Alex said dryly. "You're not fleecing Regan."

"Fleece?" she asked.

Merle shrugged his shoulders. "I just meant a quarter

a ball. Nothing to break the bank. Just a little something to make the game more challenging."

"That sounds okay to me," she said.

"No, it isn't. You don't know my brother. Some of us inherited the honor in the family, and then there's Merle. He can smell an innocent about money at twenty paces."

"Totally untrue," Merle told her. "If you haven't figured it out by now, there's no point in listening to Alex about anything related to money. He can't add two and two and reliably come up with the same sum—"

"A massive exaggeration. My sense of mathematics is just more creative than yours—which has nothing to do with the subject at hand. I can take you in pool blindfolded."

"Hah. Talk's cheap."

"So you say. Leave Regan out of it, and I'm willing to take you for a buck a ball."

"I'm in," Regan interjected.

"There's a sweetheart," Merle approved.

"Regan, he's a no-account, amoral, greed-driven, sociopathic hustler," Alex tactfully warned her.

She chortled laughter. "Now how many times do I have to tell you that I don't need a hero? Honestly, I'm okay with this. And damn. I've got to get you two together with my brothers sometime. They're merciless teasers just like you two."

"For being such a good sport, you get to break," Merle announced.

"You sure?"

"Ladies first," he assured her, and stepped aside so she could do the honors.

"Are you absolutely sure? We could flip a coin," she offered.

"No, no. You break."

Since both men insisted, Regan obliged them. One ball popped in the corner pocket on the break, and after that she took the next six.

Alex collapsed in a belly laugh midway through the first game. She'd never heard him laugh before—really laugh—which was more than enough inspiration for her to sashay around the table and ham up the play. It wasn't hard to take either of the boys. Her dad had a ratty old pool table in the basement when she was growing up. She'd been weaned on the game.

She gave them a second chance—since they insisted— but after whipping them a second time, the clock was ticking past ten. She hung up her pool cue and waggled her fingers. "Pay up, boys."

Merle forked over the bankroll he owed. "You're an evil, manipulative woman," he announced.

"Heavens. I'm coming here more often if you're going to give me great compliments like that," she said appreciatively.

"You fed the woman dinner, Alex, and look what she did to us."

"I already knew her. You're the only one surprised she mopped the floor with us." Alex hooked an arm around her shoulder. "I'm gonna walk Ms. Hussy out to her car."

"Don't let her get away until she agrees to come back for a rematch," Merle said darkly.

Regan was still chuckling as Alex walked her outside, yet her smile slowly faded. Everything was suddenly different. She understood why Merle had stuck with them like glue. Maybe she'd made inroads into winning him over, but a woman had still badly hurt his younger brother, and Merle wasn't likely to trust her overnight. She'd loved watching the brothers' incessant bickering and teasing, anyway. They were pretty typical siblings, driving each other nuts, yet with a strong family tie of love beneath that.

Still, she hadn't been alone with Alex all evening. And suddenly they were—completely alone—and on one of those blasted, Southern, sultry nights that just seemed made for lovers. The air was as soft and dark as smoke. Ghostly moss shivered in the oaks lining the drive, and the sweet, alluring scents of roses and honeysuckle drifted from the gardens.

As they walked down the steps, the dew-soaked grass glistened in the moonlight; stars were hiding in every fold of the velvet black sky; and the tease of a sleepy, flower-scented breeze whispered over her skin. It was just one of those dreadful, unbeatable romantic nights that could provoke a winsome feeling of yearning and longing...if she let it.

She wasn't about to let it. For an instant, though, she fumbled hard for something prosaic and friendlike to say. "I wasn't sure if your brother knew what to make of me," she admitted.

"Are you kidding? You couldn't have handled Merle better in a thousand years. I may take lessons. This new overbearing busybody thing of his is a little confounding. He was never like this before—"

"Until Gwen," Regan filled in.

"Yeah. Until Gwen. But he never said a word about my love life before, any more than I did about his. I love him. He's my brother. But we're about as different as a snake and a mongoose, and neither of us ever had a habit of intruding on each other's lives before."

"You should try living with four of 'em. All my brothers are ace-pro interferers, but what'cha gonna do? You can't make 'em behave." As they reached her car, she smiled at him. He grinned back. Not one of those strait-laced formal smiles of his, but one of his lethal, slow, wicked male grins that made her toes curl and her nerves flutter like an adolescent girl's. She was thirty-three, for Pete's sake. And hadn't been the nerve-fluttering type in over a decade. Abruptly she snapped her fingers.

"Darn it, Alex—I completely forgot. We left the dishes," she said.

He raised a dubious eyebrow. "You didn't forget. You deliberately left 'em for me later. You hate dishes," he reminded her dryly.

"True. But I'd have done the mannerly thing and offered."

"Uh-huh. You gonna try and sell me swampland in Arizona next?"

Well, damn the man. The first day she'd met him, he'd been so low she wasn't sure if he even knew how to smile, much less that he'd relax to the point of teasing her. There was simply no resisting the impulse to swing her arms around his neck and kiss him.

She meant nothing more than an affectionate gesture, a reward for relaxing, for loosening up, for letting himself be happy. Yet his lips were supple and warm, hidden like a secret in his ticklish beard, and there it was again. Chemistry like hellfire. Hormones waiting to ambush her. In the blink of an eye, his taste, his texture, the scent of him, sent crazed, silly messages to her heart…as if magic really existed, as if these impossibly wondrous emotions were real—with him. Only with him.

Damnation. She thought she'd shaken those stupid fairy tale yearnings a zillion years ago.

Alex didn't feel it. She was sure. Quicker than a slap, she dropped her hands and severed the kiss and fumbled, fast and furiously, for the car key in her purse. The key search gave the best of excuses to avoid looking into his eyes. "Listen, you. I had a great time tonight—"

"Regan—"

She didn't know what he wanted to say, but she was positive she didn't want to hear it. His voice had suddenly turned quiet and low and softer than a feather stroke over her skin. In self-defense, she babbled on. "Really, thanks for asking me. And you were right—you do make a mean baked potato."

She could feel Alex's eyes on her face, but all he did was open her car door. "I told you, didn't I? And now that you know the limit to my culinary skills, if I didn't scare you off, we'll have to do it again."

"You bet. Anytime," she said lightly.

In seconds she was safely in the car and peddling down his drive for home. And there was nothing wrong with ending the evening with a swift, affectionate kiss, she told herself firmly. Friends did it all the time. She was a hands-on person; no way she could quell every natural emotional gesture—and it wasn't as if she was risking Alex's misunderstanding. He still loved his Gwen. And since his house, his whole life-style, was so contrary to hers, Regan doubted any personal or sexual relationship with her had even crossed his mind.

Minutes later she scooted in her drive, hiked into her dark house and was promptly attacked by kittens. She scooped up Scarlett and flicked on a glaring light. "You can sleep with me again tonight, Ms. O'Haira, if you just won't hog the whole bed this time."

Scarlett seemed more interested in cat treats than a bedmate. Regan listened through the whole prowling, meowing suffering-cat routine, but she was still thinking that running away from Alex would be wrong. She felt good with him—even good for him. The friendship they were developing was real. And he specifically seemed to need the kind of friend who could help him loosen up, distract him from his heartache.

She hadn't forgotten how he'd swept her into his arms the other night. Remembering still made her pulse thud, all over again. And even that single short kiss tonight...something in his searing-soft eyes made her think, made her feel, that making love with a truly honorable gentleman could be perilously, deliciously dangerous and like nothing she'd ever known.

But she'd learned a long time ago to distrust those wanton, amoral hormones of hers. Maybe it *was* the lusty month of May, but she'd quit believing in Camelots and perfect loves a thousand years ago. Losing her heart to Alex wasn't going to happen.

She was too smart to fall for him. And far too much of a realist. And that was that.

Five

Alex watched her drive away, a pensive frown grooving his brow. *Vulnerable*. When he first met her, that was about the last word in the universe he thought could even remotely apply to Regan. She was bright. Sassy. Sexy. So damn full of brassy confidence and exuberance for life that it was impossible not to catch some of that joie de vivre.

But she didn't kiss with all that bright, sassy sexiness. That fast slam of a peck replayed in his mind. It was sassy, all right—but her hand had been trembling on his shoulder, her eyes shining nervousness.

Alex couldn't understand it. He was slowly coming to understand his own virulent, violent, disgraceful response to her extremely well. She was possibly the most dangerous woman on the planet...at least for a guy who was temporarily doubting his masculine prowess and attractiveness. Regan had this terrifying ability to make him feel about sixty feet tall and capable of conquering dragons. Maybe she didn't mean to, but she just plain made him feel good about himself as a man, the way he hadn't felt since Gwen had left him.

But damnation, she'd kissed *him* instead of the other way around. No one forced her. He'd kept his hands to himself the whole evening, no matter what he'd wanted to do. But since she'd volunteered that smooch, the vulnerability she expressed bewildered him.

He was still considering the problem as he ambled back inside. The minute he opened the front door, though, the sound of clattering dishes immediately distracted him.

His brother was in the dining room. "We left all this stuff after dinner," Merle said. "I forgot all about the dishes."

"Yeah, so did I."

"The food's caked on. And she just left us with 'em. What's the world coming to when you can't count on a woman to cook and clean up after you?"

Alex grabbed some plates and elbowed through the swinging doors into the kitchen. "Maybe in the evolutionary scheme of things, it's our turn to do the dishes?"

Merle switched on the overhead light—and glowered at this heretical opinion. "To hell with that. We had this whole thing down pat in caveman times—the men went out to hunt and do real man stuff, and then, you know, just let the women take care of everything else. It worked for centuries. I'm telling you, Alex, women are screwing up the natural order of the universe. We've completely lost control."

"Uh-huh." It was so odd. Alex's gaze drifted around the kitchen—the pantry alcove and glass cabinets, the midnight blue tile counters and white floor. The room was as familiar as his own name, but it was as if he'd never seen it. Why couldn't he get that sweet, vulnerable, heart-touching kiss out of his mind?

"You *could* help." Exasperated, Merle grabbed the plates out of his hands and hustled them over to the sink. "Dammit, these plates are so crusted I don't think they're gonna come clean in the dishwasher."

"Sure they will. Just keep running 'em through a bunch of times. Sooner or later the food'll give up."

"I suppose we could soak them," Merle muttered.

"And face that in the morning?"

"God, you're right. Forget that. And hell, if the dishwasher doesn't get 'em clean, maybe we can just throw them away and start with a new set."

"Hmm."

Merle stopped sorting plates into the dishwasher and glanced at him. "I said, maybe we could just throw away this priceless set of Great-Gram's hand-painted china. Heirlooms. History. I expected you to wave a knife in my face. Are you asleep over there?"

"Hmmm."

Merle abandoned the dishes and abruptly, shrewdly studied his face. His tone changed. "She's sure one potent package of energy," he mentioned casually.

"Yeah, she is."

"I haven't heard you laugh like that since I can remember. I mean even before Gwen. She's full of hell."

"Yeah, she is," Alex echoed vaguely.

Merle yanked on the light over the counter, then restudied his brother's face with the additional illumination. "It was a little hard not to notice that she had a figure that could inspire a monk. Even being a fanny connoisseur, I'd have to give her a ten...and you know I don't like to give out that rating unless the evidence is damned compelling.''

"I didn't pay any attention," Alex said crisply. "But just once in a blue moon, you might want to notice something about a woman besides her physical appearance.''

"I'll be damned," Merle murmured. "I keep telling you there's more to notice in a woman than her mind. Don't tell me there's finally one that made you think of something besides 'respect'?"

"Are we going to do these dishes or talk all night?" Alex said irritably.

Without looking away from his brother's face, Merle dumped a handful of silverware in the dishwasher. "You know, you've never brought any woman around remotely like her. She's sure nothing like Gwen.''

"Nothing at all," Alex agreed.

"And she's completely not your type.''

"I could have sworn I already told you that. Several times. She's a friend. And becoming a seriously good friend. That's all she's looking for. That's all I'm looking for. You're wasting your breath with the teasing. There's nothing else going on.''

"You sure about that?''

"Dead positive..." Alex lost the thread of the conversation again. He lifted a glass and recognized it as the brandy snifter that Regan had sipped from—it was easy to identify as hers, because the edge had a lipstick print. He found himself staring at the heart-shaped scarlet lip print, and thinking, *You've got to get a grip.*

He had to quit thinking about her this way. He'd always been a romantic, always liked every part of loving a woman, from the teasing to the wooing to the savoring power of pleasing a woman in passion. Until Gwen's defection, he'd never had a reason to doubt his ability to satisfy a woman. But with Regan, those needle pricks of doubt were full-scale daggers. He had to be nuts to think of falling in love with her. She was a sensual, sensuous Lorelei to her fingertips. He wouldn't have a clue how to please her.

And the thought of failing her rammed a tight feeling in his chest. She *was* vulnerable. She'd been hurt by men before. And dammit, he wasn't going to be another of her long list of so-called heroes who'd turned out to have feet of clay.

"So it's okay with you?" Merle asked.

Alex twisted his head. "Sorry, I was wool-gathering, didn't hear what you said."

"I said, since you're so dead positive that you and Regan are just friends, would you mind if I asked her out."

Alex snapped to. "Over my dead body. Forget it, Merle. Completely. I mean it."

"Ah," Merle murmured.

"What the hell is that 'Ah' supposed to mean?"

"Nothing. Nothing at all." Merle lifted his hands in a peace gesture. "I got the message loud and clear. No problem. Are you, um, gonna see her again?"

"That's strictly up to her."

Regan figured it was strictly up to her whether she saw Alex again. These days, both genders comfortably pursued friendships with the opposite sex, but Alex…well, Alex had some exhaustingly archaic values about women. If he sensed she was the slightest bit unsettled around him, she was positive he'd never call. She didn't want to push more of a friendship on him than he wanted, either, but she'd thought it through for several days...particularly, how to keep the door open if he wanted someone to talk with. Without being intrusive.

And this seemed a pretty good way. Teenagers jostled her as she poked her head in his classroom. Wednesdays she had no classes in the afternoon, so it was easy enough to catch his last hour of class.

Alex wasn't initially there, but kids started pouring in, strutting, laughing, chewing gum, slamming books. The high school boys were all at the gorilla stage—long arms and big feet that had grown before the rest of them. The girls were either slouching to hide their new figures or puffing out their chests to show off their wares. Some were honing their flirting skills, some dying of shyness. Regan remembered too well that whole painful era. For all the big attitudes, they were still of an age to innocently believe in happily-ever-afters.

There was only one empty seat in the last row, and she slipped into it just as the bell rang and Alex strode in. She thought she was concealed amazingly well behind a chunky brunette with big hair, but somehow he cocked his head and spotted her right off. His eyes met hers and took a long, cool drink of her. Drat the man, but his smile plugged straight into her feminine hormones.

"Before we get started, class, I want to introduce you to Ms. Stuart." Thirty pairs of eyes immediately turned to pounce on her. "Ms. Stuart is a teacher, too. In fact, she has such a personal interest in the study of historical heroes that she gave me an idea for class today. Isn't that right, Ms. Stuart?"

He knew darn well that was a total fib, but because his class was watching, Regan gravely nodded. And then leaned back to see where the rogue was going with that start-up.

"All right, now... All term we've been talking about

heroes from classical times through the Middle Ages. But today I want to give you a riddle. I'm going to give you some clues and information about a man. The first person to guess who he is, raise your hand—and you get an extra credit A for the day. Ready?''

Lots of nods. They were ready. Regan folded her arms. So was she.

''This man wasn't a hero, in the traditional sense of the word. He was never president, never won any Olympic medals, never fought in any famous battles—and as far as academic credentials, he never even finished high school. He was born in 1901 and served in World War I as an ambulance driver. After the war, he started his business life with a sum total of forty bucks in his pocket…and a bunch of wild, idealistic dreams that made some wonder if he wasn't a few scoops short in his Raisin Bran. Anyone have a guess who he is so far?''

Heads shook. Alex glanced at her. She shook her head, too.

''So you need a few more clues, huh? Okay. He was no scientist, but he made things come alive that had never been alive before. He never had anything to do with politics, yet Eisenhower awarded him the George Washington medal for being 'an ambassador of freedom' for America. In fact, by the time he died in 1966, he had more than seven hundred awards from all over the world. He was praised for having 'the unfailing professional devotion to the things that matter most—human dignity and personal responsibility.' Another said he was a 'masterful, creative leader in communicating the hopes and dreams of our free society to the far corners of the planet.' Surely someone has a guess who he is by now?''

Still more head shakes and frowns. Alex checked Regan's face again. She had to shake her head again, too, blast it.

"You guys want a real easy clue? You not only *know* who he is. You all love him."

Alex hammed up a look of despair when the class didn't pick up on this. For Regan, though, he had a fast, sneaky wink.

"Now all term we've been defining *hero* by a pretty limited set of parameters—military heroes, political leaders, guys who'd saved someone at great risk to himself. This man didn't do anything like that. He was a hopelessly idealistic dreamer—but he had the courage to turn those dreams into reality for the rest of us. He was a giver, who loved to give other people pleasure and joy. He represented America all over the world in a way that no one else ever has or ever could. Wherever he went, people loved him." Alex tugged on his beard. "I'm *still* getting no takers? Sheesh, you guys are really slow today. Does the name Mickey Mouse ring any bells?"

A dozen hands promptly shot up, and groans and shouts of "Walt Disney" echoed around the room. Regan had to grin. He really had the class in the palm of his hand—although a pixie-sized redhead in the front row couldn't wait to register an exuberant protest.

"Mr. Brennan, that isn't fair. You tricked us. I think you should give us all As because you threw us off by using somebody from today. I mean, all we've been studying is guys from the Middle Ages—"

"Yeah, I know we have...but you kids have been yawning for the last couple days. I figured you were getting bored with castles and Crusade stuff, weren't you?"

Violent agreement on that one.

"So that's why I threw in Disney today." Alex leaned back against his desk. "I know it's hard to imagine what you could have in common with folks who didn't have cars or VCRs or MTV...but you do. Life-styles were different. *Things* were different. But people were really no different from now. There were unsung heroes, people reaching out, people you'd love to know...hey, there was probably a nontraditional hero like Walt Disney somewhere in their time, even if we didn't know his name. Y'all hear me?''

They nodded, and Alex followed through with a discussion until the bell rang.

The redhead snuggled her books to her chest and aimed straight for Alex after class. Regan could smell the crush from the back of the room. Poor baby. All the symptoms were there—the rapt attention, the clumsily dropped book, the agony of nerves.

Regan waited with arms folded until the youngster finally left and Alex strolled to the back. "You've got a mean streak, Brennan," she accused him.

"Yeah?"

"I'm impressed. You give a helluva lecture. But using Disney for an example as a hero...that was a low-down, dirty trick. Cripes, even a hard-core feminist has to give a couple of inches for Disney."

Alex waggled his eyebrows. "No. Don't tell me I finally found a hero you believe in?"

"I admit you'd have to be a turkey not to love Disney. But—"

"Aw, hell. I knew there'd be a *but*."

"But he did do all those Snow White, Cinderella thingamabobs where the girls sang 'Rescue Me' incessantly to their princes. At least Snow White got it partially right. She taught those silly seven dwarfs to clean up after themselves."

Alex chuckled and then motioned his head toward the

doorway. "If you want to see a guy sing 'Rescue Me,' watch me duck behind your back if Jenny comes back in the class."

"Ah. The redhead with the big blue eyes?" At Alex's expression, Regan chuckled. "If you weren't aware, she stared at you through the whole class. I had the feeling that you could do no wrong, that every word you said was a pearl, that—"

"Would you quit teasing? I've done everything but stand on my head to discourage her." Alex raked a hand through his hair. "Do you have any suggestions? Seriously?"

Regan sobered then, too. "I didn't mean to make fun—I could see she's really got a painful crush. But I also watched you with her, Alex. I thought you were doing fine." So like him, he'd been chivalrous. Kind. Gentle. Patient. She could so easily picture him with a houseful of children.

For just an instant she felt his eyes on her face. Thoughts of children promptly flew from her mind. In a roomful of desks and cheerful sunlight and nice, normal prosaic things, she suddenly thought of midnight and moonlight and him naked in that big, lonely bed of his. She wondered what would happen if he lost that infinite patience. She wondered what crazy, outlandish magic was in his eyes that kidnapped her common sense and ransomed it for such high, wicked stakes.

"Somehow," he murmured, "I'm not getting around to asking why you stopped by. Was this just retribution— you were getting me back for sneaking into your class the other day?"

"Yeah. Mostly. I don't have any classes on Wednesday afternoons, so sometimes I pop over to the tennis courts at the college and see if I can pick up a game. But it seemed like a lot more fun to stop by and pick on you," she said mischievously.

"You play tennis, huh?"

"Not competitively or anything. I just enjoy it as a way to unwind, to do something physical after sitting in a classroom all day." She hesitated. "Do you play?"

"Well, I know one end of a racket from another, but that's about it. Still, if you're maybe up for a game..."

Something about his phrasing struck a déjà vu memory chord. Hadn't she said something about barely knowing one end of a pool cue from another at his house? But that thought quickly fled from her mind. A tennis game just seemed like an ideal thing to do. Fresh air, sunshine, a public place—she couldn't get in any trouble. And the exercise would be great for Alex, she thought, the kind of total stress release that would get his mind off Gwen or anything else that was troubling him.

An hour later she was considering murdering him.

It was hot and humid. So hot, so sultry humid, that they had their choice of tennis courts because anyone sane in North Carolina was holed up behind air-conditioning somewhere. Worse yet, all the courts were in full sun, and having baked all morning, the clay tops were shimmering heat like a desert mirage.

Regan slipped into a rest room to change into cutoffs and a T-shirt, thinking that she'd definitely go easy on him. When she came out, Alex was already unzipping his racket.

He'd changed, too. The vague thought drifted through her mind that she tended to think of Alex as an idealistic, intellectual bookworm. A man of theory more than action. A man of ideals and dreams more than an actual doer.

One look at his legs permanently annihilated those illusions. Heaven knew why it hadn't occurred to her before that he was athletic. Obviously he couldn't get that mean, lean muscular build slouching in a library chair, but the man in tennis shorts still damn near took her breath. Silly-looking knees, but the legs were long, tanned and muscular. A loose white shirt showed off the rippling cords in his upper arms and iron-flat stomach.

He turned to her with a smile as brilliant and innocent as all that dazzling sunshine. "You ready? How about a volley for serve?"

"Alex, if you're counting on a good game, I really need to tell you that I only casually play—"

"Me, too. In fact, I haven't been on a court in months. I'm really rusty."

Rusty, schmusty. The man was a killing machine. He let her win the serve, but she didn't realize it at the time. She realized plenty within the next hour, though.

She'd pinned and ponytailed her hair to get it out of the way. One by one the pins came down. In twenty minutes her T-shirt was plastered to her chest and spine. Sweat inelegantly dripped into her eyebrows. Hair glued itself to her temples and nape. And not that she'd run from one end of the court to the other, but her calf muscles were screaming for mercy.

Halfway through the second set, Alex yanked his shirt over his head and tossed it on the bench. Heaven knew why. The man wasn't even perspiring, except for a slight bead of moisture trickling from his throat down into the mysteries of his chest hair. He wasn't excessively hairy, but there were interesting swirls and sworls of patchy black-silver hair that looked as wiry as his beard. She'd have examined the issue more closely if he wasn't already bouncing back into position in the middle of the court, racket poised, a lazy look in his eyes that *now* she understood was a total scam. "You're damn good, Ms. Stuart," he said.

"Don't waste your breath on flattery. When this is over, Brennan, I'm gonna strangle you with my bare hands. Whatever happened to chivalry? Integrity? Protecting the little woman? Being kind to the more vulnerable and fragile of the species?"

"Well, hell. I could have sworn you said a hundred times that you didn't want a hero—"

"I don't, I don't. You try throwing the game, I really will strangle you. I'm gonna beat you fair and square, buster."

She lobbed her meanest, fastest serve. He returned it right past her ear. She played for blood. He never even had to move fast. She really didn't give a damn about losing, never had, and since she tended to do everything in life whole hog, the joy was in the doing no matter what the outcome. But the unsettling thought kept nagging on her mind that his Gwen wouldn't be doing this.

His Gwen likely played tennis in one of those cute little white skirts. Alex had just implied so many times that his Gwen was a paragon. Regan couldn't imagine the woman without perfect hair, immaculate makeup; and positively his ideal woman couldn't possibly have sweated. Much less like a pig.

Alex roared with laughter when she *finally* aced a serve against him. And she started to feel better. For sure, she had no trouble getting him to laugh, and it was easy to see he was having a good time. Although she couldn't play well, God knew she could play exuberantly. It was a game between friends. Exactly what it was supposed to be.

She didn't want to fall in love with him. And doing things like this, Regan mused, was just solid common sense. Because Alex couldn't possibly think, even for a second, that she was anything like his ideal, perfect Gwen.

Six

"**Y**ou dog. You let me win." Regan pointed a French fry at his face as if it was a cocked gun.

"Did not."

"Brennan. You know—and I know—that you were blistering the court with me. I was totally outgunned. Until you pulled that turkey hero move and let me win."

"Did not." Alex grabbed a napkin from the dash of his Jag. He wasn't precisely sure how they'd ended up having take-out burgers in the front seat of his car in the deserted high school parking lot. At the time, it seemed logical. He'd driven to the tennis court, which meant she needed a lift to pick up her car from the high school. En route, they both decided they were starving, but Regan insisted on takeout because she refused to be seen in public after their tennis game.

He'd already critically looked her over. Her hair *was* a little wild. And personally, Alex thought that the male population of Silvertree didn't really need to see Regan in those fanny-cupping cutoffs or that drooping-off-the-shoulder T-shirt, either. Otherwise, she looked her usual sensual, earthy, voluptuous, testosterone-rattling, sexually intimidating, heart-threatening self. Nothing different that he could see—except for the ketchup on her cheek.

Thankfully he'd brought extra napkins. She'd started out curled up against the passenger door, but it was clearly a mistake for her to try eating and fighting at the same time. He leaned over to wipe off the blotch of ketchup, ignoring the ferocious indignation in her eyes.

"Just admit it, you low-down worm. You let me win. And while you're at it, let's go for the full confession. Tennis isn't the only sport you play now, is it?"

A cautious response seemed wise. "Well, you know how I feel about teaching. But sometimes inspiring the future heroes of America can be slightly…exhausting. It's helpful to have a physical outlet now and then—you know, like racketball, swimming, softball, riding, skiing, mountain climbing—"

"Oh, for Pete's sake. You've been a closet jock all this time and you didn't let on? And you expect me to believe that you just got tired at the end of the game?"

"You outplayed me fair and square." Hell. Now she had ketchup on her chin and a little mustard, too. "Just so you know. No other woman ever made me feel like a criminal for being a gentleman before. Listening to you, you'd think I'd committed murder. Since when is being a nice guy a hanging offense?"

"Aha! So you admit you let me win!"

Amused, Alex leaned back against the window. "You think I'm dumb, Ms. Stuart? I ain't admitting nothin', nohow. But if it'll get me back in your good graces, I'll take you on in another match sometime."

"Deal." When she discovered her carton of French fries was empty, she peered over at his. "You didn't save me any?"

"I had no idea you had the appetite of an elephant, or I would have," he said dryly.

"Did you play tennis with Gwen?"

His pulse picked up—a sudden, uneasy beat. From the beginning, Regan had never hesitated to bring up Gwen, and he'd never lied or tried to duck the subject of his ex-fiancée. But this time her question really seemed to come out of nowhere.

He studied her, trying to guess what she wanted to know, or how his ex-fiancée had suddenly intruded into the conversation. But Regan's eyes were lowered for that instant. She was busy bunching their leftover dinner debris in the white takeout bag, then tossing it in the back.

Watching her, for the oddest moment Alex felt suddenly acutely aware of their surroundings. The only other car in the black asphalt parking lot was hers. No bodies were anywhere around. Clouds had been slowly, ominously slinking overhead, a bright afternoon turned murky gray, the humidity so thick you could almost taste the coming rain. Leaves rustled in a restless breeze, echoing his own edgy heartbeat. He tried to imagine doing anything so goofy or impulsive as having fast food in a high school parking lot with Gwen and couldn't. It just never would have happened.

"Yeah, I played tennis with Gwen," he answered her.

"And was she good?" Those hazel eyes were tilted to his now, but Alex still couldn't guess where she was leading.

"She could hold her own on a tennis court. She had the form, the moves down pat. She practically grew up on the game." And he'd believed she loved it, Alex mused. Until he'd seen Regan play. Regan...could be klutzy. Sometimes clumsy. She tried some wild, bold moves that were doomed to fail—and did. But every single move she made was passionate, exuberant, squeezing every ounce of life and fun from the game that she possibly could.

"Alex...are you still feeling the same way you were weeks ago? When you talked about feeling lost? You still feel like your life's turned upside down and you can't find an anchor?"

"Not exactly." Alex scratched the back of his neck. There was another fascinating difference between the two women, he thought darkly. Gwen had been restful. Regan could bluntly, mercilessly dig at an open sore—and look a guy straight in the eye while she was doing it. "I tried to explain before. I was so sure of her. So sure of the relationship. We knew each other a long time before futures or weddings ever got brought up."

"I know. You told me that before."

"We agreed. On everything. Same foods, same hobbies, same values. I can't remember ever arguing with her. She was nine years younger than I was. For a long time I believed she was too much younger, maybe didn't know her own mind, her own heart. But in everything, we just seemed tuned to the same channel."

"And now?" Regan probed.

"Now it's fairly obvious we weren't even tuned to the same universe," Alex said wryly. "You asked me if I still felt turned upside down—and the answer is, I sure as hell hope so. Obviously I needed some shaking up. It's no small screwup, to be that sure of something and then discover you were dead wrong. I don't want to make the mistake again. Or any mistake remotely like it."

"Alex..." Restlessly Regan curled a leg under her, her

face intent. "I've never heard you say a negative word against her. You're pretty hopeless with that kind of chivalry—I understand that. But you have some really strong ideas about what love is supposed to be. What you want it to be."

"What's that supposed to mean?"

She lifted a hand in a helpless gesture. "I just mean...maybe you fell for an ideal of love—a woman who seemed to fit into that ideal—instead of the real thing. Because I know from my own life, anytime you idealize something, it's hard to see what it really is. But you have to know in your head she wasn't remotely perfect, Alex. For Pete's sake, she took off with another guy. That makes her a total jerk in my book."

"You don't know anything about this, about her—" His tone turned sharp. The accusation stung, that Regan thought he didn't have the judgment to separate the real from the ideal. Possibly because that same beesting had been festering in his mind for weeks now, as he groped to understand why his relationship with Gwen had failed. Confusing him further, the more time passed, the less he felt loss and the more he felt relief that Gwen was gone from his life—which seemed to speak to how badly he'd misread the nature of love between them. But self-honesty was one thing, and Regan stabbing straight at the jugular of his pride was another. He cared what she thought of him, and dammit, his feelings of failure were nothing he wanted to discuss.

Typically, Regan appeared unimpressed by his glowering frown. She never did know when to quit. And instead of being intimidated by his curt, sharp tone, it just put her chin up.

"You're right—I don't know your Gwen," she said. "But you're my friend, Brennan. She isn't. You can say all the nice things about her that you want. It isn't going to stop me from wanting to scratch her eyes out. And a good friend isn't just going to automatically agree and say the things you want to hear."

Friend. Damned if that word didn't arouse another fury of frustration. He was coming to hate that word. Regan brought it up every time a conversation got touchy. When she said *friend,* everything was supposed to be okay, waters smoothed, intrusive subjects excused, a wild tumultuous embrace in a doorway forgotten.

Only Alex hadn't forgotten that embrace. He hadn't forgotten any moment he'd touched her. Or she'd touched him.

A splashing plop of rain suddenly hit his shoulder, then another and another. The bunched charcoal clouds overhead growled a warning. The storm was going to be on them any second now.

Regan was momentarily diverted the same way he was. She whipped around to start cranking her window closed. He jerked around to close his. Their shoulders accidentally bumped.

Both jumped back as if burned, but their eyes suddenly collided with each other. Maybe it was the rain. Maybe it was that luring, vulnerable awareness in her soft eyes. But he'd been telling himself from the day he met her that these touches were accidental.

Horse patooties. That whole denial game had worn thin.

No touch between them had ever been accidental.

Alex had been an honorable man his whole life. He didn't feel an ounce of honor anywhere near her...and no, he wasn't proud of himself for yanking her in his arms. He was plain, old mad at her. Aggravated at her probing, miffed at her analyzing him. A man never touched a woman when he was mad. That was cut-and-dried.

But nothing—not one blasted thing—seemed cut-and-dried when he was with Regan.

She shook him up. Just like she was shaking him up now. When he hauled her across his lap, her shoulder bumped against the steering wheel, but she didn't protest. His mouth slammed down on hers like a conquering pirate staking his claim—disgusting caveman behavior—but she didn't protest that, either. It wasn't how he treated a woman. Ever.

Her lips parted under his with a silky, whispery groan as if she'd been on fire, waiting for this. Waiting for him. He gulped in air and came back for more, this time claiming her tongue. Neither of them had completely closed their windows. Rain splashed his neck, started drubbing and drumming on the windshield in silver iridescent streams. The sky had quickly turned bleak black and mean. He needed to be driving her out of the storm—not creating one—and he was damn old to be necking in a car.

Only he wasn't necking. If threatened at knife point, he couldn't swear he knew honestly what he was doing—but it wasn't necking. Between the steering wheel and gearshift, there was no maneuvering space for either of them. Yet his palm slid to her throat, felt the frantic pulse, smoothed over the pale white skin under her loose-necked T-shirt.

The feel of her collarbone inflamed him. Hell. Everything about her inflamed him. The lush perfume her skin gave off as it warmed. Her yielding mouth. Those sassy hazel eyes, not so sassy now, turning soft and dazed.

A jagged streak of lightning illuminated her eyes and pearled her skin, and then fog steamed the windows so thickly that all he could see was her. Another kiss sealed them closer, tighter. She only had one arm free, but her fingers found him, first touched his arm, then clutched, then looped around his neck like a lariat drawing him down for another kiss.

He stroked the length of her, from the lush edge of her breasts, to the nipped wedge of her waist, down to the rounded curve of her hip. Then back up, skimming under her T-shirt this time. She was wearing a white sports bra. Three hooks. Alex could have sworn he was reasonably dextrous. But not now. He fumbled and bumbled, as frustrated as a teenage boy with no finesse. Yet her breasts spilled into his hands when he finally untrapped her, her skin like hot satin, the tips hard as stones. A shiver trembled through her that couldn't possibly be caused from chill. The car was hotter than an oven.

So was she. Her tremulous response was like a fantasy, like a man dreamed a woman would respond to him, sometime, somewhere, as if she couldn't help herself, as if nothing mattered but him in the whole damn universe. All her blunt honesty and gutsy confidence...it wasn't that Alex doubted they were real, but this Regan was real, too. She knew heat. He wasn't positive she knew tenderness. Because she seemed as shaken and lost and sucked into the same ferocious tidal wave that he was.

Thunder crashed. Bullets of rain pelted the windows and roof. Wind hurled leaves and debris, and still he kissed her. Still he stroked and caressed the sweet mound of her breast, the swollen tight nipple. She twisted, trying to get closer when there wasn't a breath of spare space for either of them to maneuver, and every restless, frustrated move she made rubbed her hip evocatively against the teeth of his zipper.

His arousal had teeth of its own. He was beyond hard.

his hormones growling impatience, but this need to touch her was beyond anything he could explain. Teasing her, teasing himself seemed downright crazy. It *was* crazy. He tried to put Gwen in his mind—which should have been a guaranteed way to inspire an instant quelling of desire—but Gwen wasn't there. Not her face, not her memory, not any part of her. There was no one there but him and Regan.

Rain beat on his neck. It didn't stop him. A cramp hit his thigh where she was cutting off circulation. He wanted her to cut off all the blasted circulation she wanted. That didn't stop him, either. But in one restless, frantic movement her elbow cracked against the gearshift, and she gave a sudden involuntary yelp. Her eyes popped open as if sanity had slapped her.

Sanity didn't slap him quite as quickly, but even in those smoky, shambling moments, he recognized she was hurt. "Regan...are you okay?"

"No. Yes. No." She sucked in air. "I hit my funny bone. You know how that hurts? And I don't *care* how it hurts. Damnation and tarnation, Alex, are we both completely nuts?"

In a split second she focused. On the torrential rain, the car, the parking lot...his eyes. Alex was unsure what she read in his face, but something in his expression made her bolt, and fast. She awkwardly scrambled from his lap with the speed and grace of a stampeding moose. Not that she wasn't a beautiful, unforgettable moose in his view, but the heel of her hand clopped in his thigh and her head cracked against his chin in her indelicate hurry to get to the other side of the car.

He saw stars from the chin smash. He'd been seeing magical stars moments before, too, but not quite of this type. By the time his vision cleared, she was all curled up and glued against the passenger door.

Soothing her was his first masculine instinct, but his lips parted to say something and never got the chance. Regan started talking, babbling full speed and faster than a mountain brook in a spring thaw. "Look, everything's okay. Nothing really happened, so don't even think about feeling guilty or upset. You're lonely, I'm lonely, and both of us have been celibate for a while—put those ingredients together, and naturally you've got the recipe for chemistry. We just didn't realize it was going to be this much of a problem, but now we know. There's absolutely nothing to feel even remotely worried about—"

"Whoa." Alex needed to catch his breath, even if she didn't. The thought prowled through his mind that she'd done exactly this before. Excused him. Absolved him of any responsibility and dismissed what happened as if TNT chemistry were an everyday event for her. "Regan, take it easy," he said softly.

"I *am* taking it easy."

"Your elbow okay?"

She quit rubbing it instantly. "It's fine now."

But she wasn't, he thought. The look in her eyes was tense and wary and scared...which made him feel as if he was slogging through emotional quicksand. He just didn't know what to say to reassure her. "You just want to forget this," he said carefully.

"Of course I do. I'm sure you do, too. And, dammit, Alex...we've been having some great times together. I feel like we've both been building a serious friendship that's good for both of us. I *don't* want to do anything to goof that up or spoil it."

He hesitated.

"I *know* you feel the same way," she pressed.

A rumbling shudder of thunder made her head jerk up. His eyes didn't budge from her face, but he used the distraction for what it was. "What I know," he said, "is that we both need to get home and out of this storm. And the way those clouds are moving in, I'm afraid it's going to get worse before it gets better."

"You're so right..." It was all the excuse she needed to grab her tote bag and pelt out of his car and cross the blacktop to her own. The drenching rain soaked her in those few seconds. He watched until she was inside her car and started the engine. Once she'd backed out of the parking lot and disappeared from sight, a pent-up sigh whooshed from his lungs.

Slowly he turned the Jag key, listened to the engine purr...and then just sat there.

Adrenaline was pumping through his veins as if he'd just narrowly avoided a disaster. Maybe he had. Neither honor, truth nor loyalty had inhibited his desire to make love with Regan. He almost had, and never mind what an acrobatic feat that would have been in the Jag's front seat. He'd never had a problem with self-control before. Or character. None of the values that ruled his life seemed worth more than mushed spaghetti anytime he was near her.

But Gwen was a problem of an entirely different dimension.

Alex raked a hand through his hair, aware that Regan must believe his heart was still tied to his ex-fiancée— or she wouldn't bring up the subject of Gwen so relentlessly. Ironically, memories of his ex-fiancée were usually the only thing that effectively pushed his Stop button. But not for the reasons Regan thought.

When a woman left one man for another man's bed, Alex told himself that a plague of self-doubts were inevitable. What guy wouldn't question his prowess and skill as a lover under those circumstances? But that plague of doubts turned epic size anywhere near Regan. He'd never please her. Never. She was so tuned to her emotions, so naturally sensual and earthy. He could all too easily picture her with a lusty alpha male, but no way could he imagine a nice-guy, gentleman type inspiring her between the sheets.

And a fist squeezed tightly around his heart at the thought of failing her.

Alex hadn't forgotten that she'd been failed before. By men who hadn't met her needs, who'd failed to be there when she'd needed them. And maybe he was confused why these compelling, powerhouse sexual feelings kept springing up between them, but he wasn't confused about caring. He cared about her. Deeply. Deeply enough to recognize that all Regan's flamboyance hid a fiercely, impossibly, vulnerable woman.

Maybe she didn't believe in heroes, but Alex had considered, more than once, that she might be coaxed to believe in love again—if she found a man she could seriously trust.

Frustrated, his thoughts as murky and tumultuous as the storm, he shoved the Jag in gear and aimed for home. A man friend could do that for her. Be a good guy. Be a man she could seriously trust. But, dammit, not unless he kept his hands off her. Making love risked more than his own failure—he'd be risking Regan if it didn't work out.

And that was out of the question. There simply could be no more "accidental" touches, he mentally lectured himself. And that was that.

Scarlett and the kittens scattered the instant she opened the bottle. "You don't like the smell of hair dye, huh, guys?''

Regan slipped on the plastic gloves with the skill of an experienced surgeon. Twenty minutes from now she'd be a new woman. A redhead.

It was a ploy she'd tried before, and it always worked brilliantly. Change the hair color, change the woman. After her first run-in with kissing a frog—her senior year in high school—she'd tried going blond. She'd been a brunette for six months after her breakup with Ty. She'd tried some subtle streaks after—well, it was best not to remember that occasion. Thankfully her hair grew fast for those coloring experiments that had been a teensy bit less than successful.

When she'd finished squishing in the hair dye, she checked the time, then lavished a minute studying herself in the mirror. The view immensely satisfied her. This wasn't a woman Alex could love. It was a woman ready to audition for the starring role in a grade-B horror movie.

Naturally the monster was going to disappear when she washed out the gook in a few minutes, but what the hey. Regan was well aware the ploy was psychological. Who cared? Sometimes a startling change gave people an effective whomp upside the head. She needed some kind of startling, realistic whomp after throwing herself at Alex in that damn car—in the middle of a thunderstorm yet.

There were some other disgusting signs that she'd fallen hard, deeply and painfully for Alex...like she'd never fallen for another man. She knew the pattern, though. Next thing, she would be dreaming about him, miserable every second when they weren't together, believing in fairy tales and happily-ever-afters—in spite of all the bold-print evidence that Alex wasn't even remotely, conceivably for her. *Something* had to firmly slam that silly, irresponsible door her heart had sneakily opened up.

She was going to make herself behave as a redhead. And give herself some breathing space to get her new red head together as well.

The plan came together over the next few days. The hair-color ploy not only worked like a charm, but the looming end of the school term guaranteed a busy stretch. She had exams to prepare for, a faculty tea, a summer seminar to organize. Just teaching and life chores kept her running. But her spirits were up, and her attitude rerooted in realism.

On Thursday afternoon she took a break and charged into Cookies with three of her students after class. Cookies was predictably packed—the campus hangout was always jammed by mid-afternoon. The place smelled like chocolate and coffee, favorite addictions for both teachers and students. Regan's gaze skimmed past the rough-pine paneling and green leather booths, seeing familiar faces and bodies everywhere—but no spare seats.

Julie, one of her sophomores, grabbed her arm and surged ahead. "Come on, Ms. Stuart, I see a table just emptying out. And then you gotta finish telling us about those idiot men and that genius story again."

Regan knew what she was referring to—the class hour had abruptly ended when she was right in the middle of a story, and her three most ardent feminists were hot to discuss it. She just couldn't immediately answer Julie. A harried waitress jogged over and took orders, and it took a few minutes to get everyone settled. Regan had plopped down her briefcase and purse, pushed off her shoes, and had her hands wrapped around a mug of almond-raspberry coffee when she opened her mouth to start the discussion again. And abruptly closed it.

Alex was across the room. Stretched out in a booth with two men friends, fellow teachers, judging from the mound of papers and notebooks heaped on their table. He was wearing an innocuous, conservative, button-down shirt—so like him, so unlike her—and his eyes were crinkled at the corners as he chuckled at something one of his compatriots said.

One look at him and her heart started up with that ooga-booga rhythm thing. He hadn't touched her. Hadn't even seen her. Damn her untrustworthy heart. Particularly after that debacle in the thunderstorm, her heart had been trying to convince her that he'd never really been in love with Gwen. Not like he thought. He couldn't possibly love Gwen—not real love—and respond to her with such giving and passion and fire.

Alex glanced up as if his attention had wandered from the conversation with his teaching pals. His gaze dawdled around the room, drifting en route past the faces at her table. He paused at the dark-auburn redhead in the wild print jumpsuit…then passed on. Again he said something to one of his friends.

Regan tugged at an earring. It was almost funny, that he hadn't instantly recognized her. The change in hair color was never meant to be a disguise, nor had she any intention of hiding from him. She'd just wanted to give herself a slap of a change.

Her heart had a long habit of selling her wooden nickels. The reality of the situation was that Alex was on the rebound—horny and hurt—both perfectly human feelings; but no intelligent woman stepped in front of a moving train. Any woman in his path right now was simply a substitute for Gwen.

Truth to tell, Regan recognized his masculine esteem was pit low because of Ms. Jerkess dumping him, and she refused to feel guilty because they'd let some chemistry get out of hand. If it upped his confidence to realize another woman found him compelling and sexy and desirable, then Regan was just glad it was her making him feel good.

Nothing actually *wrong* had happened. Apart from the teensy problem with combustible chemistry, they worked wonderfully well together as friends. The only thing that could screw that up was if she did something damn stupid like fall in love with him....

Alex suddenly looked up from his cronies again. His gaze pounced straight to her face.

"Ms. Stuart, are you awake there? You didn't answer—"

"I'm sorry, Julie..." Regan zipped her attention back to the girls—never mind that her pulse was cavorting like a colt's with spring fever. Swiftly she gulped a fast slug of coffee. "I just couldn't quite hear you over all the noise—"

Faith leaned closer, folding her arms on the table. "Right at the end of class, remember? You were talking about Roman mythology, Juno and Zeus—"

"Right, I remember." The jolt of caffeine worked. She picked up the subject. "Juno was the Roman queen of the heavens. In that time period, she was basically considered the 'woman's god,' because one of her jobs was to watch over all her daughters on earth. So for a long time, *juno* became a common symbolic word. Every woman was a juno. It just became the term used to mean a woman's soul."

"Yeah. But now get back to the part about the guys." Julie had her arms folded on the table now, too.

Regan's gaze darted back to Alex, but temporarily her view was blocked. So many bodies were milling around that she couldn't see any of the back booths at that moment. "Well, in those Roman times, *genius* became the common symbolic word to mean a man's soul. Originally that was a natural pairing for the *juno* term, because the base of the word *genius* meant begetting father."

"So genius didn't automatically mean anybody who was, like, superbrilliant the way it means now. The word just meant *guy*. A guy's soul," Faith echoed.

"Exactly. Only the Roman Empire failed after that. And patriarchal societies took over and reigned for a bunch of centuries. And somehow while the guys were in charge, the boys retained the word *genius* to idealize the male...and just happened to accidentally forget the corresponding word *juno*."

"Men! If that isn't a typical rat-fink male chauvinist move," Julie said disgustedly.

"Using any excuse to put us down. Controlling us through laws, through physical force...even through language—"

Julie, Faith and Priss were the most militant feminists in her last-hour class, which was partly how Regan got embroiled in these after-class discussions with them. Their thirst to learn pushed all her teacher's buttons, but sometimes encouraging them to think through their set views was more than a little challenging.

"Well," she said, "I think that's one way to look at it—man as a woman's worst enemy—but I tend to believe it always took two to tango. Part of what I've been trying to show you in all the fairy tales and myths we've studied this term is how we women have persisted in treating men as heroes. Superhuman beings. We expected them to take care of us, protect us, shelter us—"

"Ms. Stuart! You're saying it's okay they thought of themselves as geniuses and dropped our juno thing like we didn't matter at all?"

"I'm saying," Regan said patiently, "that whether or not we like it, maybe men weren't entirely responsible for such things happening. If we expected men to be heroes, maybe we expected them to be more than human, more than fallible...more than they could be. And if they treated women like 'lesser' human beings, it was possibly because our own attitudes through the centuries fueled their power—and their belief—that it was okay to treat us in a no-account way."

A hand closed on her shoulder. A big, warm hand. Up, past the hand, past the expanse of a blue oxford shirt, was a dry smile hidden in a roguish beard. "This sounds like a terrifying discussion for a man to interrupt. Can I say hello or would I be risking my life?"

Seven

Regan cupped her chin in a palm. Sheesh. It was so pitiful. Her rabid feminists...the three most dedicated, militant, hard-core man-eaters in all of her classes...had turned into eyelash batters faster than a finger snap. Faith had smoothed her hair. Julie hadn't quit with those shy, seductive smiles. Priss had pushed back her chair and crossed her legs—displayed in the season's shortest skirt, no less.

It was like watching Rome fall from a sideline seat.

Alex didn't even *do* anything—besides pull up a chair and look adorable. Well. Once he heard a replay of the whole Genius-Juno discussion, he promptly, chivalrously, took the blame for his entire half of the species.

The truth was, Regan thought glumly, she was just as inclined to bat her eyelashes at him as the girls. But someone had to maintain decorum at the table. Her three budding feminists kept sneaking her glances. *Is this your guy?* they silently asked. Regan had the distinct, disastrous feeling they were seeing orange blossoms and china patterns in her future. It was the same old story. The girls were dead positive they were antimen—until a cute guy crossed their path, at which point they were positive "true love" would win and happily-ever-afters would instantly ensue.

Teaching them to *tch-tch* at the fairy tale had always been a lot easier in theory than reality.

Alex murmured, "Was it something I said?"

"You mean because the three of them suddenly took a powder faster than fillies at the Kentucky Derby? No. They freaked out because they thought we wanted to be *alone.* So we could discuss glassware and china patterns and the important things in life."

"Uh, beg your pardon? China patterns?"

"China patterns are a female ritual thing," Regan patiently explained. "I thought it died out a couple of decades ago, but then I came to live in the South. It's still thriving here. Basically china patterns are a critical nesting symbol. You haven't *really* hooked your man until you've tamed the beast into dutifully trailing after you in a store to pick out china patterns."

"Possibly this conversation is too intellectual for me, because I'm still not getting it," Alex said dryly. "Your girls split at the speed of sound because of something as incredibly convoluted as china patterns?"

"Give or take." Since she was looking for an excuse anyway, she batted her eyelashes at him. "They thought you were courting me. That you're my guy. That they were interfering in a 'true love romance' by hanging around."

"Ah." Alex's eyes danced with humor—and a darker glint of something less fathomable. "Okay, got that. Now could you give me a clue how the conversation leapt from the God-can't-you-just-hate-all-men discussion to true love romance?''

''Damned if I know. It seems to be something that women do. Worse yet, it always seems logical to us. That's what's so frightening. Sometimes I think there's just no solution except for all of us to come back in the next life as men.''

''No, no, you don't want to do that. I like you just the way you are.''

''You mean illogical? Contradictory? Batty?''

Alex couldn't hold back a chuckle. ''Hey, I always thought logic was way overrated. The world would be incredibly dull if everyone behaved the same way. Unpredictable is fun. And speaking of unpredictable changes...it took me a couple seconds to recognize you, but I really think it's beautiful.''

''What?''

''The red hair. It suits you. Although brunette seemed to suit you, too. Did something prompt the change?'' His gaze roved over her red hair and wild print jumpsuit.

His comments were gentlemanly, she mused. They always were. But the way he looked her over made her think of marauding highwaymen and pirates. Alex never seemed to notice that she didn't fit in the land of Laura Ashley and big hair. He never seemed to notice that compared to his buttoned-down style, her eccentric clothing choices should have clearly illustrated that the two of them were never meant to be a matched set. His real problem with perception, Regan thought, was his entire lack of interest in clothes. He had this gift for stripping a woman naked with his eyes.

Her throat felt the brush of his gaze. Her mouth felt the caress of his touch. The straggly strand of hair bounc-

ing somewhere around her temples felt his eyes posses-
sively smoothing it back as if his hands had actually
touched it.

"Regan," Alex repeated, "was there a reason for the
new hair color change?"

Yeah, there was a reason. So she'd quit doing this.
Imagining harebrained romantic feelings for Alex, where,
dammit, the poor man didn't intend any. She'd hoped the
symbolic physical change would whomp her into shape.
Toughen her up. And it had seemed to be working brilliantly—until Alex got within two feet of her.

"I just got tired of brown hair. And it seemed like fun.
How'd your teaching day go?"

She'd meant the casual question to change the subject,
which worked just fine. Only it was a little bewildering
how she ended up at his house a short time later, popping
TV dinners into his oven and scrounging in his cupboards
for napkins and silverware.

The thing was that they always had a good time talking
together—as long as hormones stayed out of it. And once
they naturally started talking, neither really wanted to end
the conversation, so it just sort of traveled with them to
his place. Regan even realized it was her fault. She'd
come up with the idea of Alex playing visiting teacher
for one of her fairy tale classes…he could do a male
viewpoint lecture thingamabob on the subject of heroes.

"You'd do that to me? Make me walk into a room
with all those women? I thought we were friends. It'd be
different if I owned a bulletproof vest or a full suit of
armor."

"Now, now. My students may tend to be a tad on the
feminist side, but they're all ladies. You want the sick-
looking meat loaf or the sick-looking chicken?"

"Which TV dinner has the peach cobbler?"

"The meat loaf."

"Then I'll take the meat loaf, unless you want it. And as far as your ladies, I'm not real inclined to being lynched alive."

"They'd love you," Regan assured him. "Furthermore, they need to hear it from you. A man. That believing in the fairy tale hurts both genders. Fills both sides with unreasonable expectations that affect their understanding of relationships—yikes, I burned my tongue."

Alex pushed her glass of water closer. "Clearly you're not a TV dinner pro. You have to wait at least five minutes. Although there's some advantage in burning off your taste buds before you've really gotten into the meal—"

"Quit trying to change the subject, you turkey," she gasped between gulps of water. "I think you'd have fun, lecturing to my girls. Seriously. I think it'd be great for them and fun for you—"

"Um, Regan, you don't seem to realize that I don't agree with you. I think a woman has every right to expect certain things from a man—especially her man. Love. Honor. Honesty. Loyalty. To be protected and cared for. The whole fairy tale shebang."

"Holy kamoly." Regan shook her head disgustedly. "What am I gonna do with you? Have none of my lectures gotten through? This entire hero theory simply has to go. Men get the same short end of the stick as women do by believing in the fairy tale. Look at King Arthur."

"He's been dead awhile. It's pretty tough to look at him."

"Now don't get smart with me, you." She threatened him with a fork. "I've said it before and I'll say it again. Guinevere tossed out the best man she was ever gonna find in a lifetime—and all for a stud running around with tights and a sword. I'd call Guinevere a shallow nitwit, except that she only followed through with what she'd been taught. What Arthur in fact taught her. That some stupid ideal of true love was more important than reality."

They'd been down this road before. She knew this was a touchy subject for Alex, but darn it, a real friend did more than dispense attaboys. It always seemed to Regan that he'd been hurt exactly as she'd been hurt herself in the past, by interpreting seismograph hormone activity for what it wasn't. Still, she should have expected Alex's eyes to turn cool and his expression to mask up on her.

"Regan," he said irritably, "she loved someone else, for Pete's sake. That *was* Arthur's reality. If Arthur couldn't fulfill her needs, she was justified in finding someone else who could—"

"Horse patooties. She just had a lust attack for a face man with a big sword. If you ask me, Arthur was lucky she took off. He could have been stuck with the shallow, stupid woman for the rest of his life... Merle, could I see that *Wall Street Journal?*"

Merle, just passing through the kitchen to grab a drink, had the day's paper tucked under his arm. "You're a *Journal* reader?"

"No, but I haven't had the chance to turn on CNBC for a couple of days and wanted to check on some stock prices."

"I'll be damned. I'd have figured the two of you for the last financial virgins on the planet—no offense, bro. You're into the market, huh?" he asked Regan.

"I can't say my portfolio is extensive, but I dabble some." She checked her Disney, then swiftly folded the paper and handed it back to him.

"Is that 'dabble some' on a par with how you play pool?"

Before she could answer Merle's question—and she guessed an invitation for a pool match was coming—Alex intervened. "No, we're not up for a pool game tonight. Did you get that glass of water you came in for?"

Merle retrieved the empty glass he'd abandoned on the kitchen counter, industriously filled it with water, and then seemed to forget about it again. "Possibly I heard raised voices in here and thought Regan might need saving from a fight...furthermore, Regan, if you're looking for a *good* argument, you could come up to my lair and we could talk about stock options and futures—"

"Um—" Regan cleared her throat "—I'd love to do that. Another time. But I promised Alex that as soon as we finished dinner, I'd seduce him on the piano top in the living room. It's a point of honor thing. You know how strong your brother is on that, and I really don't want to risk doing anything to jeopardize my hussy reputation."

Merle slapped a hand over his heart. "God forbid, neither would I. And not that I'm doubting for a second that either of you plan to follow through with this wild, wicked plan for the evening, but should you need advice, interference, a voyeur in residence—"

"Good night, Merle," Alex said.

"Good night, Merle," Regan echoed.

"Hey, I can take a hint. In fact, I was headed out for a couple hours to see a friend. But if you'd give me your absolute promise that you won't behave while I'm gone, I'd feel a lot better about leaving you two alone—"

"You have my word I'll do my best to get your brother in trouble," Regan said gravely, which earned her a clap on the back and a grin of approval.

Once Merle was gone, she glanced at Alex. They both chuckled and then quickly scrambled to their feet. Once the TV dinner plates were tossed out and silverware popped in the dishwasher, the cleanup was done. "I'm going to be hard-pressed to give you any trouble. I can't even remember what we were arguing about now," Regan grumbled humorously. "And I suppose I should be heading home. It's already pitch-dark, and I still have a briefcase of papers to grade."

"I have a mountain of work still to do yet, too, but...do you like music?"

Her eyebrows arched at the question. "Sure."

"I was just thinking that a few minutes listening to some music might help settle dinner."

"Sounds fine to me."

Regan assumed he meant listening to a stereo or radio or something like that. Even when he ambled toward the living room, she didn't guess he meant to play the piano. Merle had clearly told her that Alex only played for himself, never company. And her nerves skittered uneasily when he strode toward that wide, black, gleaming-hard mattress of a piano top after her joking with his brother.

She was ninety-nine percent positive Alex never had a second thought about that joke. Still, her eyes shot to Alex's face to catch his expression. The sun had long set, though, and with no lamps on, the room was so dusty-musty dark that she couldn't really see his face clearly. He didn't switch on a light...just plopped down on the piano bench and immediately launched into an exuberant boogie-woogie.

She chortled laughter. "You think that kind of music is gonna help us settle dinner, huh?"

"You're right. We need something older. More traditional," he said thoughtfully, and instantly switched to a foot-tapping ragtime that made her laugh all over again.

"You're wonderful," she enthused.

"Had five years of piano lessons forced down my throat as a kid. They had to be good for something. Come on closer. It's a lot more fun if you can feel the music. Pop on top of the piano or I'll move over to make room for you on the bench. You have any favorites?"

"Not really. I like pretty much everything." Again Regan felt a flicker of uneasiness at his reference to the piano top, but really, that was foolishness. She needed to settle somewhere. Just standing there while he played felt awkward, and she really didn't want to listen from a chair or couch way across the room. She hesitated—snuggling hip to hip with him on the piano bench was just asking for trouble. So, impatiently, swiftly, she hoisted herself up to sit on the piano top, thinking she was making way too much of a simple choice. "Go for it, Brennan," she said with a grin.

He did, and she easily forgot that moment's uneasiness. The blurry duskiness gradually turned into a true velvet darkness. Alex didn't seem to need light, either to read music sheets or even to see the keys. He kept her chuckling with his eclectic choice of music. He thundered into Beethoven's Ninth, whisked into some low-down bluegrass, then bounced into Brubeck's old "Take Five."

Slowly, though, her smiles started fading. At first it seemed accidental that his innocuously varied choice of music included some love songs. But there came a point when that was all he played, one after the other…lonely-heart songs and winsome, sentimental torch songs and silky, satin songs about forever lovers. Most of them were hokey. Corny. Stuff she was way too practical and realistic to believe in anymore, but damn. She never should have sat on the blasted piano, because she could *feel* the music, feel seduced, intimately, physically. She could feel the pulse and rhythm of every chord throbbing against her thighs, her fanny.

Regan had never embarrassed easily, but even in the darkness, she could feel a flush heating her throat, her cheeks. Alex was such a gentleman. She was positive it would never cross his mind that every haunting chord, every vibration, was creating a physical sexual response in her. She wanted. Him. Him of the shadowed beard and the eyes softer than a kiss and the face so pale and striking in the darkness. She wanted him as if an erotic spell had trapped her in its cobwebs. She wanted him as if every hokey, corny lyric in those love songs had been written for them. She wanted him so badly she could taste it.

"Alex. I have to go." Her voice came out shrill and sudden and loud. She couldn't help it.

As if he'd almost expected to be interrupted smack-dab in the middle of a song, he immediately lifted his hands from the ivory keys. "Of course you do. And I never meant to get carried away and play for so long. I've got tests to correct, and I know you said you had work waiting, too."

"I do. I do."

But before she could leap down from the piano top, he stood up from the bench and hiked in front of her. He'd moved so fast she was startled—but only for a second. Heavens, she mused, Alex was just being Alex. He obviously intended to help her down.

Only he didn't lift her down. He stepped between her thighs and wrapped his big hands around her waist. He pulled her closer, so close that his pelvis was resting against her abdomen, and even in that pitch-black darkness, his mouth found her mouth.

The whole thing was an accident, she thought. He couldn't know how badly she wanted to jump him. He couldn't know that forbidden, erotic thoughts were chasing through her mind out of control. He couldn't *know* a damn thing....

But he took her mouth. Not as if he was offering an affectionate goodbye peck. But as if he was on fire and he wanted her burning with him. As if he'd suddenly taken up ravishment as a spare-time hobby. As if he wanted her, now, fast, hot, naked, rough.

His tongue dove into her mouth and never came up for air. His beard tickled, teased against her soft cheek. His palms curled around her fanny, cupping her tight, making her pelvis rub hard and evocatively against him. She'd made love. She could have sworn she knew all the dangers of hormones, could have sworn she'd dismissed passion as something nice, yeah, but best kept a lid on until she was sure, damn sure, of her guy.

She wasn't sure of Alex. She'd never been sure of him. Instinctively she'd first judged him a good man, a special man, and coming to know him had hugely and irrevocably affirmed that trust. But she'd never fathomed at all what he felt for her, beyond seriously and honestly needing a friend. Especially lately, no matter how she tried to keep the subject of Gwen open, somehow Alex seemed to avoid expressing where he stood or what he felt for his ex-fiancée.

Regan was scared she was only a substitute for the woman he really loved. And just as scared that Alex wouldn't normally be attracted to a woman like her if he weren't lonely and hurt right now. But this chemistry between them kept happening. And, tarnation, kisses

from Alex were so damnably power-packed that she
couldn't think, couldn't slap any common sense into her
mind, couldn't remember all the brilliant, sensible reasons why this was a terrifyingly bad idea. When she was
with him, everything in the whole darn world seemed
right.

The front door slammed open.

The sound came from the distant hall, but still it reg-
istered in her mind: Merle was home. And unless one of
them exhibited some sign of sanity immediately, Merle
was going to find a shameless hussy with her legs
wrapped around his brother closer than peanut butter on
bread.

Regan reared back her head and said hoarsely, "I'm
going home, Alex."

"I know you are." Alex sounded calm. And amenable.
But he dipped right back for another kiss. This one was
deep, dark, wet. His tongue was softer than magic, and
after a long, sipping taste of mouth, he sampled the length
of her long, white throat.

She swallowed. Her voice still came out with the volume of a frog croak. "Alex."

"Hmm?"

"Right *now* I'm going home."

"I know you are." Again he sounded calm and amenable. But this time his hands squeezed her waist and he
simply, smoothly, lifted her down. Her feet connected
with solid ground, terra firma, but her knees were shaky
and every nerve in her body was rattling like tin cans in
a high wind.

"I really *am* going home," she announced, and then
realized she'd repeated that statement and conceivably
could continue repeating it indefinitely. There was no
point trying to talk when nothing was coming out but

blather. She took a step away from him, then stumbled toward the door.

Even recognizing that her current state of mind resembled a train wreck, she felt even more bewildered when he didn't try to stop her, didn't say anything. She didn't know *why* he'd kissed her at all, not that way, not starting something so deep and wild and unstoppable. What grown man invited that kind of physical frustration unless he intended to follow through? Yet for all her belief in bluntness and honesty, she couldn't ask. Even assuming she could have gotten the words out, she wasn't positive she could handle hearing the answer.

Merle was still in the hall, battling with the door and two hefty brown sacks of something or another. He started a greeting, then took one look at her face. "Hey, everything okay? You need a ride home?"

The poor guy. He had no way of knowing that anyone in her path right now wasn't going to get anything more coherent out of her than more blathering. "No, my car's right here. I'm fine. Everything's fine. Life's fine. Good night, Merle."

Alex had his feet up in a lounge chair, red pen in hand as he corrected history tests, when Merle wandered into the library a couple of hours later.

"I conjured up some chocolate chip cookies. You want any?" his brother asked.

"Does the sun rise in the morning?" When Merle produced an entire platter from behind his back, Alex regarded him suspiciously. "What's my ration?"

"Have all you want. I was hungry for 'em, so I got a bunch of extra ingredients. Easy enough to make more." Merle waited for him to choose one, still steaming, with the chocolate still melting soft, and then carried the platter over to the leather couch. "So…what the hell did you do to her?" he asked amiably.

"Do to Regan?"

"No, I mean the woman in the moon." Merle scowled at him. "Of course I mean Regan. She left here galloping at a thousand miles an hour, no lipstick, babbling nonsense, hair styled by a tornado—"

"Ah, well. You don't know Regan as well as I do. She never stays looking neat for long. Bring up something as innocuous as the weather, and she's bouncing and waving her hands. She just tends to do everything in life energetically—"

"She had her top unbuttoned."

Alex regarded him over the sea of history papers. "It was probably just a loose button."

"Uh-huh. You want another cookie?"

"Not if I have to take the grilling along with it. There's nothing to report that you'd be interested in. We had a quiet evening, talking, played the piano for a little while—"

"You played the piano for her?" Merle hunched over. "You never played for Gwen. Hell, I've never heard you play if you knew for sure anyone was in the house—including me."

"It was just a whim. Even die-hard conservatives are entitled to a whim now and then. And no kidding, Merle, I've got at least another hour of work to do before I can turn in, and it's almost midnight now."

Merle took the hint and left, taking the chocolate chip cookies with him. Alex focused on the history papers for another half hour, then quit. His vision was blurring. For a moment he leaned back in the chair and rubbed his eyes, thinking he was beat and should hit the sack.

Faster than an ambush, a picture of Regan stole into his mind. There went his last thought of rest.

He lurched out of the chair, slugged his hands in his pockets and hiked outside through the French doors. The long sweep of lawn was smokily lit by a white satin moon. Crickets called for their lovers. The scent of roses and honeysuckle was heavy in the air, and his bare feet were soaked from dew before he'd walked ten feet.

The memory of her mouth haunted him. So, tarnation, did her body. Every inch. Breast, hips, elbow, throat, wrist. In his adolescent years he'd considered himself a leg man, but with Regan that sort of thing was irrelevant. The tip of her little finger could turn him on. And, dammit, regularly did.

She thought he was still in love with Gwen. It clawed his conscience, painfully, that she'd think he would come on to her if his heart were still attached elsewhere. But he didn't know how to say aloud that he was afraid to make love with her...afraid of not satisfying her, of not being exciting enough to please her, for the "now" or the long term. And Gwen at least temporarily stood between them like a nice, handy, coward's excuse. Regan wasn't going to let anything go too far as long as she still believed Gwen was an in-house ghost.

Alex never planned for anything to go quite that far, either. It was the music that did it. Watching her shadowed face, her eyes, as she listened to the love songs. A young girl's yearning had been in her soft eyes. Yearning, longing, need.

She didn't believe in love—she said. But he'd come to see that she was afraid to believe, afraid of being hurt. And that wasn't the same thing at all as not believing.

He admired her strength and respected her realism, but he thought she badly needed a dose of magic. Wonder.

The emotion of love as he knew it. Because—right or wrong, sane or insane—that was undeniably what he felt for her. And the way she responsively ignited in his arms, Alex had the crazy, confounded feeling that she'd never been exposed to the real thing. No matter how many so-called heroes had run through her life, she seemed stunned and unprepared, lost when he touched her. Heaven knew, he couldn't have done anything she wasn't familiar with. And probably he hadn't done anything all that well or excitingly in comparison with any other guy.

He'd just…shown her what he felt and couldn't say. He'd just…loved her.

Abruptly he spun around and clipped back toward the house. A bramble lodged between his bare toes. He hopped up, yanked it out and scowled as he hit the steps toward the French doors.

He refused to be another man who failed her. But to not show her honest love…damned if he wouldn't. He could be careful, infinitely careful to make sure nothing went too far. But how was she ever going to work past those fears if she never met a man she could trust, never experienced those emotions with a man who seriously cared for her?

Brennan, you are in so far over your head that you may never get out.

Maybe her realism was catching, because his heart heard that clear warning. And possibly that warning was true for him. Maybe he was doomed to be unendurably hurt by this. But she wouldn't.

There was no way he would do anything to hurt Regan.

Eight

Regan's gaze strayed to the phone on her bedside table, but she firmly averted her eyes back to the open book on her lap. She read two paragraphs, none of which made a lick of sense, then glanced at the phone again.

Scarlett O'Haira chose that moment to leap on the bed, followed by the hellions. All the hellions now had vampire-length claws and no good ideas. Technically they were old enough to give away, but who'd want 'em? All of them had psychopathic personalities with no conscience. Scarlett galloped past Regan, clearly seeking to escape her beloved children, but as she aimed for a protected perch on the beside table, she accidentally knocked the phone receiver off the hook. It practically fell in Regan's hands.

"Would you cut it out?" Regan grumbled. "I'm telling you I have the guts to call him. I'm just not ready yet. I need a little longer to think about it."

Scarlett had heard a variation on this theme for several nights now. She settled down on her haunches with a wary eye on her children. But as soon as Regan replaced the receiver, the cat nuzzled it off the hook again. This time it crashed to the carpet.

Exasperated, Regan reached down to retrieve it. "Listen, advice from you isn't worth a wooden nickel. That was always your namesake's whole problem—pining after Ashley Wilkes. If Scarlett hadn't gotten the stupid idea that Ashley was her 'ideal hero,' she'd have been happier from day one. Grown women don't *pine*. And they don't lust after men they can't have. They kick themselves in the fanny and get over it."

Scarlett, into this game now, nosed the receiver off the hook again the instant Regan hung it up.

"Oh, for Pete's sake. All right, all right, I'll call and get it over with!" The kittens had taken up sniper positions from behind every mound in the bedcovers. Regan pulled the sheet over her head to dial.

The phone rang once. Then twice. As she waited for an answer, her mind dispensed a mantra of warnings. *Speak normally. Don't mention pianos, whatever you do. Sound cheerful. Sound happy and friendlike. Sound...*

"Alex here."

Well, hell. If there was a man with a sexier baritone on the planet, she didn't know him. Her mind instantly replayed a dozen telltale images from the other night. Her legs wrapped wantonly around him. The "yes please" invitation she must have mortifyingly communicated with her abandoned response. His eyes in the darkness. Eyes that seemed to touch her soul—if she believed in such nonsense. She swallowed hard and forced herself to push the Stop button on those mental replays.

"Hey, Brennan. I'm calling to hound you. I know

we're both coming to the last two weeks in the school term, and you have to be as busy as I am preparing for finals and all—''

"You know it," Alex commiserated.

"But I was still hoping you might be able to come play visiting teacher for my last-hour fairy tale class. I know you laughed when I suggested it. But I just mean one hour. And I think you'd have fun—you *know* how you feel about heroes—and I think it'd give my girls some fuel for thought to hear a man's perspective on all the stuff we've been talking about. That Thursday class of mine doesn't start until four in the afternoon—''

"Yeah, I could do it—as far as being able to arrange the time. But that doesn't solve the bigger problem. Seems to me a guy could mightily risk losing life and limb walking into one of your classes—''

"No, no, I'd protect you from the ladies." She twirled the phone cord around her hands, starting to smile. It felt like the first real smile she'd indulged in in days. "Think of it this way. This is your chance to get your licks in. Wouldn't you like my darling, violent, radical, militant feminists to hear another point of view?''

A chuckle rumbled from deep in his throat. "Maybe. For a price.''

"Alex! I thought you were above blackmail!''

"Hey. I'm into honor, loyalty, truth, chivalry. Nothing in those rule books about blackmail.''

She faked a sigh. "Okay. What'cha want?''

"How about a drive to the coast for dinner after that class? The temperature's supposed to kick up near one hundred degrees all this week. The kids are as squirrelly as I am, between the end-of-the-term pressures and this incessant heat. I'm up for an escape.''

"Hell, I just knew you'd ask for something really awful. But I do believe I could manage that."

When she poked out from under the sheet to hang up the phone minutes later, Scarlett took advantage of the cave opening to sneak under the cover with her. They nose kissed. "See," Regan murmured, "nothing to it. I've been telling you for three days that calling him would be easy. He's a gentleman. He was never going to bring up piano tops or anything else that dicey. He'd never put a woman on the spot that way."

But for the strangest moment, Regan wished he had.

She didn't want Alex to realize she'd fallen in love with him. It was too painfully easy to imagine his finding some tactful, kind, gentle way of telling her how unsuited they were. She didn't need the rejection. She already knew they were totally unalike.

But she didn't want him ever falling for another Gwen—a woman who didn't appreciate him, a woman with a roving eye. A woman who'd hurt him. And that was ample motivation for Regan to continue pursuing a friendship. Once he was past Gwen, past being vulnerable over that hurt, maybe she could force herself to see this differently. But until then, her being in his life was a way to protect him from further hurt. No matter what heartache she was risking, Regan couldn't see that a real friend—a loving friend—could do less.

On Thursday evening the blacktop road to the coast was all but deserted. Regan had one hand on the wheel, the other trying to hold back her hair. The drive was wildly windy, and her air-conditioning wasn't functioning well enough to close the windows. The temperature was frying hot, but she didn't care about the heat or the wind. She'd invested buckets of worry in this outing with Alex, all for nothing. It couldn't possibly be going better.

She was still laughing at how well the devil had taken on her Thursday fairy tale class. Alex had stood up there, looking meek and shy and adorable, hamming up the image of the "helpless male" at the mercy of a lecture hall full of females. "Ms. Stuart made me do this," he had told all of them. "Your prof challenged me to come up with a hero in some fairy tale that really epitomized an ideal—at least from a man's point of view. So I did. But I'm really not sure we're all gonna agree on this."

Neither were her girls.

"Y'all know the story of 'Rumpelstiltskin'?" he'd asked them. The girls started nodding with curious expressions. That definitely wasn't one of the fairy tales they'd covered in the course. "Okay. We've got a damsel in distress, trapped and being blackmailed—she's going to lose her life unless she can get the infamous straw spun into gold, but the only one who can do that gold trick is Rumpelstiltskin. And she's supposed to pay up—in the form of giving up her firstborn child—unless she can come up with the jerk's name."

Regan was still chuckling, remembering how he'd smoothly turned that tale into a lesson.

"Well, she's it, ladies. That damsel in distress is a true hero in my book. When she's confronted with evil, she does what she has to do to survive and makes no apologies for it. But when threatened with further evil, she shows resourcefulness and courage. She steps up to the plate to save herself—and her baby. As an ideal hero, she strikes me as pretty classic. She rescues herself. Not with might or violence—she doesn't kill anyone. In fact, she harms no one in this tale—she simply uses her character and her brain to outwit the forces of evil. This is a hero of honor and courage and strength to admire...who doesn't need a sword to win. She wins solely because she's a human being of high principles and integrity."

Regan checked her rearview mirror for traffic—and then shot Alex a glowering look. "And to think I never realized how sneaky you were. Good grief. You weaseled out of trouble in that lecture as slippery as a greased pig."

"You're calling me a pig?" Alex sounded wounded.

"You know damn well the girls were expecting you to come up with a *man* hero!"

"Hey, you didn't tell me I *had* to talk about a guy. Although I have to admit, I practically had to pull an all-nighter to find a fairy tale I could use. There do seem to be just a few where the swashbuckling knight shows up on his white charger to save the princess. The girls don't exactly get many stellar action roles in those old stories."

"See? See? What have I been telling you!"

"I see, I see." Alex cleared his throat. "But does this mean I can't save a damsel in distress if I come across one when I'm riding my white horse?"

"That *means,* you doofus, that occasionally you have to let the damsel save *you.*"

Alex raised an eyebrow. "You think I have a problem with that? Take note. You're driving. You brought the dinner. I'm napping in the passenger seat with my feet up. I like this 'being saved' business just fine. Either that, or you've successfully turned an archaic male around to your brilliant way of thinking."

Regan gave him credit for being a retrainable archaic male, but right in the middle of that teasing banter, she discovered that there seemed to be a couple of archaic female patterns that she was nastily prone to herself.

She found the turnoff road to the beach with no sweat.

She couldn't have been more in favor of his idea of driving to the beach after class. It was only an hour's drive. The whole week had been blistering, mean hot. A picnic at sunset and a cool-off dip in the Atlantic struck her as an unbeatable idea. No dishes. No fuss. Cool off and relax for a couple hours, then drive home.

That was the plan. Regan just forgot that plans with Alex tended to go awry. He was a man to value the ideal—yet around him, she seemed doomed to have every personal flaw show up in spades. She'd embarrassingly sweated in their tennis game, cracked her elbow in his car in the middle of a kiss, babbled incoherently when she was shaken up; hell, they'd even met when she dropped books in his lap. Tonight was even worse.

Somehow she thought his Gwen never would have allowed this to happen. When she parked her Mazda on the beach, the waves were thundering in and spitting out debris. A hot, blustery wind was tossing sand. There was no sun in sight—no imminent storm, either, but the dreary, gray skies and wind alone had driven most beachcombers to scoop up their stuff and head home.

She plucked a blanket from the trunk. When she tried to shake it out to make a tablecloth, it plastered right back in her face. The wind was kicking up enough sand to season her potato salad. A plastic cup took off before she could pour the first drink.

"Maybe we should have tried a picnic dinner in a nice, quiet air-conditioned room?" she said dryly.

"Hey, we're still escaping from civilization. And it's a meal with no dishes."

"There's always that," she agreed. Rightly guessing there would be no place to change, they'd both worn bathing suits under their clothes. She charged to the shore to dip her toe in the water and shook her head, then shouted, "Well, it's warmer than Lake Superior. But then, ice is warmer than Lake Superior."

"That's where you swam where you grew up?" Alex asked when she returned to the blanket. He'd taken charge of setting out dinner—and bolstering anything that wasn't tied down with rocks.

"Sometimes. There are freshwater lakes everywhere you turn in Michigan. Most of them are so cold you could get instant hypothermia, but there's definitely no shortage of places to swim."

"This coast has its share of hurricanes."

"Tornadoes are more the thing in Michigan." They'd both lived through one herculean encounter with nature, and as they inhaled dinner they compared the terrors of hurricanes versus tornadoes. Devouring the food fast was their only option. The wind whirled her hair every which way, took off with the napkins and threatened every container with sand and grit that she tried to open.

Naturally, the blasted, contrary wind died—as soon as they were done trying to eat. Still, as they stretched out together on the blanket for a few lazy minutes, Regan mused that nothing was really going that badly. He laughed about their bad luck with the weather. So did she. Whenever they were together, they never had a problem talking easily, endlessly. And like now, they'd always seemed to be able to relax together—the way only real friends could.

"Have you heard any more from that Ty since you moved down here?" Alex asked her.

She turned her head. With his arm behind his neck and his eyes closed, she'd thought he was catching a catnap. For sure the question about her ex came out of the blue, not that she minded answering. "No. But I didn't expect to."

"Hmm."

"What's that 'hmm' mean?"

"Nothing, really. It was just on my mind, how that guy took off on you when he believed you could be pregnant. And from other things you said, you've really run into more than your share of men who let you down. Have you thought about why?"

"Of course I've thought about why. I started out with expectations that men were like heroes in the fairy tales. If they swept me off my feet, it must be love. Thankfully, enough experience finally taught me to be realistic."

"Yeah, I know your views on that, Ms. Realist. But somehow I keep thinking about those guys. And how, maybe, a certain type of man might especially have gone looking for you, sugar."

"What do you mean?" Regan propped up on an elbow.

"I mean that you're strong. And you come across as full of hell and confidence—which are incredibly fine qualities." Finally he turned his head and opened his eyes to look at her. "But strength can also be a defense, Regan. You could give a man the impression that you can handle anything, with both hands tied behind your back. Possibly that's the impression Ty had of you. And, possibly, that was the only picture you ever gave him, the only one you wanted him to see."

Irritably she blew a strand of hair from her eyes. The fitful breeze whipped it right back. "Alex, I don't have a clue what you're driving at."

"I'm just trying to say that before you turned down the sheets for the night, you must have noticed that your character was a ton stronger than his. He was a jerk. He left you in the lurch. That's not your fault—it's totally his. But you're a damn bright woman, sweet pea. So I'm wondering what you were doing with a guy like that."

Alex, she reminded herself, was a gentleman. He would never attack a woman. He would never put her on the spot. "Obviously I didn't know what he was like ahead of time."

"No. But maybe you specifically weren't looking for a hero. If you were serious about a guy," Alex said peaceably, "seems to me that you'd go into the relationship feeling the right to make certain demands. That your guy be faithful. That he step up to the plate when there's a problem. That he's a man you can let down your hair with. That you can trust him."

"For Pete's sake, Alex. Obviously I want those things in a relationship. Who doesn't?"

Alex didn't seem to hear the rising defensiveness in her tone. He simply, gently, answered her question. "Maybe a woman—or a man—who feels safer when they're with a weaker mate. I can see that'd be a way to protect yourself. You don't have to reveal anything vulnerable—or risk getting naked, so to speak—with a guy you don't really care about."

She hunched up. "You're saying I'm responsible for Ty being a jerk? As if I deliberately chose to be with a turkey?"

"You're mad at me," Alex announced.

Heavens, no. She felt hurt. Aggravated. Testy. Ready to growl at the nearest seagull. But certainly not mad. "I'm guessing you're leading somewhere with this, so just continue," she said curtly.

Her tone was sharp enough to cut rock. Alex's, by contrast, was calm and warm and quiet. "I'm just wondering if you ever picked a man you actually wanted, Regan. That Ty, for example...do you miss him, wish you were married to him, still wish he were part of your life right now? And of course I recognize that he hurt you, but I'm still asking…is there a chance that you were glad, if not relieved, to see him go?"

Regan felt as if he'd picked off a scab and revealed a raw sore. Alex was right that she'd never found it easy to reveal her vulnerable side to a man. And maybe she did give most guys the impression that she was strong and tough—a woman who could handle anything. But, tarnation, once you kissed your first frog, it was hard to admit out loud what you were scared of. It was the same as giving someone else the power to hurt you.

She'd just never put that together before, the way Alex's nasty perception put unpleasant questions spinning in her mind now. Had she really never looked for a hero? Been unconsciously picking weak suckers all this time?

"You're upset with me," Alex said quietly.

"Not upset, exactly…. I guess I'm wondering what brought this on."

"Well, you've tried to help me sort out my feelings for Gwen so often. It occurred to me—as a friend—that I should be doing the same for you. Encouraging you to talk about things. Especially things that maybe you need to air out, but couldn't share with a friend you didn't trust."

Darn it, she thought morosely. That was the whole problem. With him, she could both trust him and talk about anything—even if she were slightly tempted to boil him in oil for making her see—and feel—things she didn't want to.

Well, that had gone over like a lead balloon, Alex thought dryly a day later. He'd never been much on psychobabble and analyzing feelings. Women seemed to love it, but most men didn't seem to have the gift. At least, he obviously didn't.

Twenty-four hours had passed since that conversation with Regan. As he parked his Jag and climbed out in Leon Bartholomew's stately drive, he considered that nothing had gone right since then. The whole day had been a bumbler. Regan was royally ticked at him—even if she hadn't come out and said it. This morning Merle had accused him of losing some sacred financial document and had gone on a long rant about the magic he'd have to pull off to fix it. The kids had been crabby and testy all day, the weather still unrelentingly hot, and the only thing that could make this day doubly bad was a meeting with Leon Bartholomew of the school board.

Alex rapped his knuckles on Leon's front door, choked the tie at his throat and schooled a smile on his face.

Leon promptly hurled the door open and clapped a hand on his shoulder. "Haven't seen you in a blue moon, Alex," he roared. "About time we caught up and had a little chat. Let's get you a bourbon and ice. We can sit out by the pool. How're you and your brother doing? Life treating you okay, son?"

Alex didn't waste time mentioning how much he hated bourbon, just accepted the glass, said hello to Marilee— Leon's saint of a wife—and allowed himself to be led out to the baking-white patio. The kidney-shaped pool was an aquamarine mirror. There wasn't a breath of air stirring for love or money. But Leon had his way of doing things, and any variation from the established program only slowed down the process. No one had ever died of heat prostration out by Leon's pool—at least that Alex knew of.

"So how has your health been, sir? And Marilee's?"

Leon launched himself in a lawn chair with a beaming

smile. Twenty minutes of the required chitchat began. Physically, Leon was white-haired and dignified, and a portly version of Colonel Sanders. The relationship was an old one. When Alex's parents had died, Leon had been one of several in the community to extend a mentoring hand to Merle and Alex, in an honorary uncle fashion. Southern manhood stuck together, certainly through deaths, births, affairs and scandals. There was no shame or sin that hadn't been done in the South and discussed over bourbon. If you hadn't done anything dark enough, the landed gentry were prepared to wait a generation or two until something meaty surfaced. Something always did. Leon's love of gossip, though, had always been tempered by his generous kindness and genuine involvement in the community.

Alex was prepared to die of sweat. Didn't even loosen his tie. Leon meant well. He'd been a shoulder for both brothers in that awful grief-stricken year when they'd lost their parents. And more than once, Leon had roared to the school board when Alex wanted something the administration tried stonewalling him on.

"That's what I really wanted to talk to you about, of course." Leon hunched forward and plucked the pitcher of bourbon and ice from the poolside table. "We're nearing the end of another school year. Like I've told you before, you're wasted in the classroom, son. You've got the power, the personality, the respect of the community. You could have the school superintendent's job in a blink. Really *do* something in that job, instead of spending all day with those ragamuffin kids."

They'd been down this road before. Not a hundred times, but it had to be close to ninety-eight. "Rawlins isn't retiring yet," Alex said patiently, referring to the school superintendent.

"He could be. If you wanted the job."

"I happen to like the ragamuffin kids, Leon."

"Of course you do, of course you do," Leon boomed, although his expression clearly showed he couldn't imagine it. "But you could do anything in this community, son. Anything. Especially in the school system, with your dedication. You could have so much more power, more influence—"

"I'm extremely fond of power, sir. A strong believer in power, in fact. I just don't happen to believe there's any job more powerful—or influential—than working one-on-one with kids."

"An idealist, just like your father," Leon murmured fondly, and then warmed up to the attack, the same way he had with Alex, Sr. in his time. Leon's favorite theme was the importance of a man's status and reputation, and he just couldn't see how a man could capitalize on either, hidden inside a classroom.

They'd snarled out this whole skein of yarn before, so Alex already knew it would take Leon another twenty minutes to wind down. By that time Leon was on his third bourbon and was no closer to accepting that one simply couldn't budge rock.

"Well, you'll think about it, son, won't you?" Leon insisted.

"I sure will," Alex agreed. Usually that courtesy comment let him off the hook. This time was no different. Leon led him back through the house, having won the only concession he ever won in these discussions, roared something at Marilee about dinner and ambled back outside toward Alex's car with him.

"I've got one other thing I wanted to tell you," Leon mentioned confidentially. He carefully closed the front door, making clear that he didn't want his Marilee to hear this, and leveled a concerned look on Alex. "I hate to be the one to bring you unpleasant news...but I feel you should know. Your ex-fiancée flew back into town last night."

When Alex didn't immediately respond, Leon seemed to assume he was suffering from shock and lifted a beefy hand to squeeze Alex's shoulder. "She's staying with her parents, I heard from Rawson Smith. And that's not all. From what I hear, she dumped that man she took off with. Ask me, I suspect she'll show up on your doorstep one of these days. Of course, it's none of my business what you want to do. But speaking for myself, I'd be prepared for the lady trying to pick up where she left off. I hear she wasn't back in town an hour before she was asking questions about whether you had any new female irons in the fire."

An hour later Alex was back in his classroom. It was after five. The only other soul in the building was the janitor, who could vaguely be heard whistling country-western tunes as he did his room-to-room cleanup. Alex slouched in his desk chair, feet propped up on the desk. He planned to head home. And soon. But just for a few minutes he wanted total peace and quiet to think.

In keeping with an already disastrously bad day, he'd already heard—three times now—that Gwen was back in town. Leon's news came as no surprise, but if Leon knew, likely anyone in a three-county radius had also heard.

Which meant Regan was likely to hear it shortly—if she hadn't already.

He heard the click of heels over the drone of the janitor's waxer...and looked up just as Regan poked her head around the door. Her auburn hair was wildly curly today, her bare legs shown off in sandals, the lemon yellow sundress dipping just a bit too low and hemmed just a bit high.

Alex's hormones started humming just at the look of her—but not because of the legs and cleavage. He noticed those. Hell, a man would have to be dead not to notice those. But sometime back, he'd picked up the harebrained idea that Regan dressed to distract a man. And when she specifically dressed sexy, it was because she didn't want him noticing something that mattered to her.

Like the carefully proud tilt to her chin. Or the fiercely vulnerable look in her eyes.

"I called you at home, but Merle said he thought you might still be here, working on exams."

"I'm about done," he said. "Not doing anything constructive but woolgathering, to be honest."

He smiled. So did she, but she didn't edge far into the classroom. "I was ticked at you yesterday," she said bluntly.

"I know you were. And I apparently blundered on your feelings with the finesse of a bull. I'm sorry, Regan."

"You don't have to be sorry with me, ever. For saying what you think. I just didn't really want to hear what you had to say. I'm thinking about it." She acknowledged that, then dropped the subject faster than a hot potato. "I need to put in about an hour or so at the library. Just wondered if you might want to pick up some fast food and go with me."

Another offer of friendship, he mused. So typical of Regan, she always made clear that no fight or disagreement meant that friendship's door was closed. She never pushed. Her attitude was always a light "take it or leave it." She'd be company if he wanted it, not if he didn't.

She'd never given him the first hint that she wanted

more than friendship with him. That she remembered all the times chemistry had hooked them both with velvet, powerful claws. That she even knew how totally and irrevocably she'd changed his life.

"I can't do the library tonight. My brother's going to shoot me until I straighten out some financial thingamabob with him. But I need to tell you something," he said quietly.

"Yeah, I had the feeling there must be something on your mind. You wouldn't still be sitting here at school this late unless something was bothering y—"

"Gwen's back in town."

She went still as glass, then promptly produced a dazzlingly bright, cheerful expression. "Well, you guessed she'd be back sometime. And I think you should see her, Alex. I don't know how fast you can create an opportunity, but probably it'd be best if you just get it done. However you still feel about her—and why ever she's back—seeing her would probably just make everything clearer...aw, *damn*."

She glanced at her bangle watch, shook it, glanced at it again and then shot him a rueful look. "I thought it was four-thirty, not after five. If I don't get going, I'll never get all the work finished I need to do at the library. Listen, I'll catch you later, okay?"

She disappeared faster than a wizard could flash a wand. For damn sure, she flew from the doorway faster than he could get a word in.

Alex clawed a hand through his hair. He'd never considered *not* telling her about Gwen. Gossip in Silvertree was such a fine art form that she could easily hear something half-baked or mightily embellished if he hadn't told her straight himself.

He'd intended a little more explanation than just a

bumbling, bald announcement, though. Regan raced out of there so fast he'd had no chance. The way she'd responded, Alex thought glumly, might easily give a man the sneaky impression that she was all for his throwing himself back in his ex-fiancée's arms.

Blindly his gaze fell on the stack of exams on his desk.

His kids had been frazzled and cranky this whole week. They always were when they felt the pressure at the end of the school term.

He particularly commiserated with that type of frazzled, frustrated pressure. He didn't want to be friends with Regan. Never had. Never would. But he couldn't balance on this tightrope forever…trying to interpret how she was in his arms, how she looked at him, how she touched him—against the clear verbal messages she sent him about "friends only."

He didn't want to fail her.

But doing the right thing—the ideal thing—never seemed to work with Regan at all. Alex seemed to bumble and fumble in masculine quicksand every time he was around her. Worse yet, he simply had no clue how to turn that around.

Nine

Regan had just come in the back door, huffing and puffing from carting in grocery sacks, when the phone rang. She plunked down the bags and her car keys and grabbed the receiver.

The caller wasted no time on a greeting. The voice was male and brisk. "I think you should come over here and borrow a cup of sugar."

Regan sputtered a chuckle. "Luckily I recognized your voice, Merle. Otherwise I'd have been dead sure this was a fruitcake crank call. Still, could you be a tad more informative on the sugar reference? You don't think I'm sweet enough? Or is this a joke, a subtle reference to my nonexistent baking skills?"

"This isn't a joke. It's a state of emergency."

"Uh-huh. Sure it is."

"Regan, just come over and borrow that cup of sugar as quick as you can, okay?"

Merle hung up on her before she could respond. He was joking about the emergency, of course, but she stared at the phone for a long, thoughtful moment...and then moved. The ice cream and frozen goods from her grocery raid were going to melt if she didn't promptly take care of them. She foraged in the brown bags, stashed the perishables, left the canned goods, then fed the cats. Scarlett was gone—doing a sleepover at the vet's while she was getting fixed—and two incredibly brilliant, fine children down the block had been suckered into adopting Henry VIII and Cleopatra. That still left Don Juan and Casanova, both of whom prowled and nuzzled between her legs as she dumped cat food in their dish.

Once they were distracted with the chow, she hustled into the bedroom. The burnt orange shorts had been good enough for a grocery store run, but they just weren't the right clothes for trouble. For trouble she dressed in a conservative navy T-shirt and wraparound madras skirt, then pushed her feet into sandals. After slapping on lipstick and a spritz of scent, she jogged through the kitchen for her car keys and headed out.

So, she thought, as she drove to Alex's. It wasn't as if Merle made a habit of calling her for cryptic little chitchats. There was only one conclusion she could possibly reach.

Gwen was over there.

Which is absolutely none of your business, announced a firm, rational voice in her mind. Not Merle's business, either. And days before, when Alex mentioned Gwen was back in town, Regan had given herself a blunt, ruthless talking-to. Only Alex could determine what he felt for his ex-fiancée. And if he didn't know that answer, it was up to him to figure it out one way or another. She couldn't help him do that. Merle couldn't help him do that. It was a job Alex had to do alone.

As she pulled into the Brennan drive, she saw the pristine, fresh-washed-and-waxed, pastel blue, new-model car in the drive. Noticeably, it was a girl car. Her stomach promptly clenched in a fist of nerves. This was so stupid. She didn't have an excuse under the sun for popping over here, and what on earth could she possibly accomplish but embarrass Alex—and herself—by functioning as a bumbling, fumbling, awkward third party?

Impatiently she climbed out of her well-loved rust heap and strode for the door, muttering swearwords under her breath. Merle's name was attached to all the X-rated verbs. He was the problem, of course. Even knowing that Merle was an intrusive, interfering busybody, he'd still shaken her up by calling. To begin with, trusting a woman was a walk on the wild side for Merle. She figured the situation had to be pretty dicey for Alex's brother to even consider picking up a phone.

If she ended up embarrassing herself, then she'd just have to live with it. Because just in case Alex *was* in a mess, there was no way she could sit home and watch CNBC for the evening without knowing for sure.

Merle opened the front door before she reached the top step. Typically he was dressed in funereal black and looked hearthrobbingly handsome—to an unbiased female eye. Regan's vision was permanently biased in another direction.

"What a surprise," he said heartily. "Come on in and I'll get your sugar."

"Cut it out, Merle," she threatened under her breath as she crossed the threshold. "And just so you know, I'm gonna strangle you alive if there wasn't a damn good reason for your getting me into this."

"Hey, you don't trust me?"

"Love you, yes. Trust you, no. You've got a little history of manipulative interfering before this."

"I'll give you bookie odds that you'll feel different after meeting her."

Regan had long guessed that Merle wasn't fond of Gwen—and felt personally relieved that her own status had been bumped to the level of trusted ally. Unfortunately, the ally status was worthless unless she had the time to grill him for details, and the front door was barely closed before she heard Alex's voice calling "Who's there?" from the living room.

"Just Regan," Merle called back.

Just Regan scowled at him and then took a long breath for courage. It was too late to back out now. She plastered a smile on her face, hiked into the living room and immediately clapped a hand over her heart. "Darn it, Alex, Merle didn't mention you had company. I just stopped by to borrow a book...you mentioned one time that you had an *Atlas of Legendary Places,* and I couldn't find a reference quite like that in the library. But honestly, I could have done this any time.... I'm really sorry I didn't call first—"

"No problem, Regan." Alex bolted off the couch, temporarily blocking the view of the woman sitting next to him. For that instant all she really wanted to see was him, anyway. She heard the warm, welcoming tone in his voice, but that told her nothing—Alex could probably manage to sound polite to a burglar. There were tired shadows under his eyes, and his expression seemed tight with strain, but he was moving too fast for her to really study him. "Funny, I don't remember mentioning that book...but you're right, I know I have several references like that. I'll run into the library and look, but first...Regan, this is Gwen Anderson. And Gwen, this is Regan Stuart, a good friend."

Merle shuffled in behind her. "I'll just get Regan a drink while you look for that research book," he offered.

"I don't have to stay. It wasn't like that book was an emergency," Regan said swiftly.

"You just got here. And it's hot. Of course you want a drink," Merle informed her. He clapped her affectionately on the back—pushing her farther into the room with the finesse of an elephant. "And, Gwen, would you like a freshener on that one?"

"Sure, sugar. Another dacquiri'd be delightful." To Regan, she said cordially, "Sit down for a minute, why don't you? I take it you're one of Alex's teaching friends?"

Alex disappeared on her. Merle disappeared on her. And not that men disappearing on her wasn't the history of her life, but that still left her alone with Gwen.

Regan had wanted a look at the woman for a long time. But now that she caught a look, she'd prefer to be on a fast jet to Tahiti. Moscow. Japan. Hell's bells, any other continent would do. "Yes," she said amiably, "I'm a teacher—an assistant prof at Whitaker in women's studies."

"How interesting. I met Alex because of his teaching, too. I was one of his students, actually.... It was his first year teaching, and I was just a junior in high school at the time. I had a crush on him from the first day I showed up in class." She smiled woman-to-woman. "Naturally, that was a long time ago. Once I grew up, our love of history brought us together.... I always could spend just hours listening to him. He knows so much about everything."

"Ah, yes. He certainly does." Regan perched on the

edge of a chair, feeling like a blowsy hound next to a groomed poodle. In principle, she'd expected exactly what she saw. The perfect princess. Blond, delicate, soft-voiced, made for pastels. Trim boobs, nothing overflowing, and no extra chocolate chip cookies on *those* hips. The skirt length was ladylike, and the baby blue eyes had swiftly done a head-to-toe assessment—not unkindly—but Gwen had clearly dismissed her as only a chance friend and certainly not a rival for Alex's affections.

Regan, of course, had told herself precisely that a hundred times. It was downright idiotic to be jealous of the pastel princess, when she'd accepted—completely—that her type of style and looks were not naturally Alex's cup of tea. And Gwen, she could see, was nice. Really nice, actually. With poise and charm, the lady continued with the chitchat, obviously making an effort to make a stranger feel comfortable with idle, innocuous conversation.

The meeting was going so nicely that Regan couldn't quite explain why an instinct of archaic chivalry stirred in her blood and sluiced through her veins in an adrenaline rush.

There was no reason, of course, why chivalry had ever been a man's domain. And this was the twentieth century—a woman could do the protecting job as well as a man any day of the week. Regan wasn't positive what spurred the violent protective instinct, but it seemed to be the cavewoman messages Gwen was sending out. Alex this and Alex that peppered her comments. She gracefully rose from the couch and roamed the room as if to the manor born. Sweet or not, Regan recognized a woman announcing her territory. *I know this house. I can touch anything I want. Naturally I'm tolerant of Alex*

*having an occasional woman friend with his work, but
just so you know who belongs here.*

Eventually Gwen ambled back to the couch, lifted the
stem of her glass and discovered it empty. "Heavens, I
can't imagine what's keeping Merle this long—"

"I'll go see!" Regan jumped to her feet. Naturally she
crossed the room with due decorum, but once she'd
cleared the doorway and was out of Gwen's vision, she
galloped straight for the kitchen.

Merle spun around when he heard her slapping open
the revolving door. "Uh-oh. Things aren't going well? I
thought you bringing up that book was a magic touch of
brilliance."

"Yeah, well, Alex is still in the library looking for that
imaginary book. And Gwen's hot for her drink."

"I'm getting it. But I decided to make a whole fresh
pitcher of dacquiris, and that takes a little time. All that
crushed ice—"

"Don't give me any dadblamed excuses, you low-
down worm. You left me alone with her deliberately."

"Uh-huh. So what'd you think?"

She ducked that. "Obviously *you* think something or
you wouldn't have conned me into coming over here."

Merle moved busily, setting out a tray, fresh glasses,
napkins. "She showed up here. No call. Took Alex off
into the living room, but I accidentally happened to be
in the hall—"

"Accidentally?" Regan sighed. "Never mind. Go
on—what'd you hear?"

"She split on the boyfriend, Lance. Said she'd realized
almost from the first moment that she'd made a terrible
mistake, never loved him. She was just shook up by pre-
bridal jitters...which, alas, temporarily blinded her to her
true feelings. She also must have repeated about ten times

that nothing happened between her and Lance that Alex need worry about..."

"Meaning she was trying to tell Alex they'd never had sex."

"Gwen doesn't use three-letter words in mixed company, but, yeah, that's the nutshell. It was damn obvious she'd come home to make a new play for Alex."

Regan leaned against a counter. "You don't like her, Merle?"

"I did," he admitted. "At first I thought she was sweet. Innocent. She hung on Alex's every word. They talked for hours. She seemed to adore him. And she never slipped from that role for a long time. But then I started to catch her doing things, like looking at the bottom of an antique plate to check the label."

Regan frowned. "So? There doesn't seem anything strange about that. She likes historical things—"

"Horseradish. She likes money. Status in the community. The influence of being married to a Brennan. And the damn thing was I could understand perfectly well why Alex never saw it. That's not how she was around him. Ever."

There was a catch in her throat. So thick she couldn't swallow well. "Look, Merle, maybe you're right on that...but that doesn't mean Alex doesn't really care for her. Cripes, this could be like an ideal dream come to life for him—his true love come back. And maybe he really does love her—"

Merle rolled his eyes. "Regan. He didn't laugh with her. He didn't moon after her, chase her around the house. She was just always *there*, making sure he was busy, no time to look at anybody else, acting like she believed everything he believed, felt everything he did.

And you've got the power to do something about this mess.''

"What the Sam Hill is it you expect me to do? I'm just a friend, for Pete's sake.''

Merle arched his eyebrows. "Then be a different kind of friend. Slip off your shoes. Take off the bra under that T-shirt. Shake your hair loose. Go in there and sit on his lap.''

Her jaw dropped. And then the tension eased out of her shoulders as a chuckle squeaked out of her throat. She sank into a kitchen chair before that first gasp of a chuckle deteriorated into a full-fledged belly laugh. "Oh, what I'd give to have that on video. That serious expression on your face while you're giving me advice on how to act like a femme fatale.''

"You think it's funny?''

"I think it's hysterical. For Pete's sake, Merle. I can do up a hussy routine—but only if it's meant in humor. If I tried that Greta Garbo act on Alex, he'd laugh me out of town—or call the folks from the funny farm.''

She grabbed a napkin to wipe her eyes. They were just laugh tears sputtering out, not sad tears...but for one brief, terrifying millisecond, they were almost both.

She couldn't compete or compare with a Gwen. That was cut-and-dried. But damn, for that millisecond...she wanted to. It had nothing to do with loving Alex, she told herself. It was just knowing Alex had hard-core, un-budgeable attitudes about honor and courtesy with women, and she was afraid Gwen would hurt him again, afraid he couldn't see there was shallowness beneath those beautiful baby blues. Merle's Greta Garbo femme fatale suggestion was total foolishness, but if seducing Alex would—

Suddenly the kitchen revolving door swished open. "What on earth are you two doing in here?" Alex asked.

"Nothing, really," Regan started to say, but Merle interrupted her.

"This hussy was laughing at the way I was making a pitcher of dacquiris," Merle said, his tone aggrieved.

"Uh-huh." Alex looked at his brother, then at Regan. "I couldn't find the one book, but the thing is, I found about six others that had the same kind of reference information. I can show you what I've got in a minute, but—" He turned to Merle again. "Would you mind taking Gwen home?"

Merle popped to attention faster than a soldier at reveille. "No sweat. I'd be glad to. Pronto. Only...I thought she came in a car?"

"She did. But she says she's having trouble with it, that the engine 'coughs' every time she turns a corner." Alex cleared his throat. "She asked me to follow her home. And I think that's a good idea—it's getting dark, and I wouldn't want her to be stranded on the side of the road. But—"

Merle was already flying for the door. "I'll do it, I'll do it. You just stay here and attack the dacquiris with Regan."

Alex watched his brother disappear—slower than a flash of lightning, but not by much. Seconds later he heard Gwen's voice, raised high enough that Alex guessed she was protesting the change in plans. But whatever Merle responded to her, Alex heard the front door close moments later. Once he was assured they were gone, he glanced at Regan with an uneasy tug on his beard. He'd heard her laughter all the way from the hall, but there sure wasn't an ounce of humor in her eyes now. "Would you like a dacquiri?"

"No, thanks, but you have one if you want. Honestly, I'm just not real fond of them."

"I never liked them, either." He hesitated. "You want to hit the library and see those other books?"

"Sure," she said.

They left the kitchen, crossed the dining room and hall and ambled past the living room toward the library. It was hardly a lengthy walk, but Alex could hear the grandfather clock ticking in the hall, the drone of a bedroom air conditioner upstairs. They were never silent when they were together. Ever. Assuming they weren't just talking about life, Regan could inspire him into a teasing argument in two seconds flat.

Not tonight. She was totally mum. He couldn't guess what she thought of Gwen—or what she'd thought when she'd walked in and found Gwen huddling next to him on the couch.

Alex must have had more frazzling evenings. He just couldn't remember any. Eventually he'd expected to run into his ex-fiancée, but he hadn't anticipated her showing up, unannounced, making a lot of noise about picking up where they'd left off. Well, hell. Whether he appreciated needing to have a rotten, blunt talk with her, a man did what a man had to do. Only there was no prayer of talking to her, because first Merle hovered like a fluttering bat—and then Regan had popped in with those huge, stricken hazel eyes.

He wasn't inclined to humiliate Gwen in front of an audience unless he absolutely had to. The talk would wait, but Alex wasn't fond of postponing unpleasant jobs, and his frustration level with Gwen, with the evening, with his brother, with life, had escalated nonstop over the last hours. His nerves were wired for sound. And being near Regan, tonight, was particularly more rattling than restful.

"Here we go." Alex jerked on the overhead light in the library. She knew the room, had nosed into his myths and legends section before this. The bookshelves were teak, floor to ceiling, with a rolling ladder for reaching the first editions. Regan being Regan, she'd never noticed the museum-value collection of netsukes, the priceless antique gaming table cum desk, the Turkish rug in almond and burgundy. She noticed books. In fact, he suspected she wouldn't notice a million-dollar cashier's check lying on the floor if there were books in the same room. Swiftly she hunkered down and plucked a couple of volumes.

"These'd be great, if you wouldn't mind my borrowing them," she said.

"Of course I don't mind." He wasn't sure what she wanted with two books on erotic practices in the Far East. But then she hadn't hunkered down anywhere near the myths and legends shelf. And she hadn't even glanced at the books.

She bounced to her feet. "Thanks a bunch. These'll really help. In fact, I'm going to head right home and start researching right away—"

"A lot of fuel for thought in both of those," he said gravely.

"And you know how much I love this whole subject," she agreed, even as she was spinning around and hustling for the door.

"Regan?" This was crazy. He caught up with her in the hall. He didn't want her to leave—much less when she was obviously upset, and it didn't take a Ph.D. to figure out that Gwen was the source of the problem. He'd never lied about his ex-fiancée to Regan, but certain mountain-size masculine insecurities had given him excuses for ducking a serious, truthful discussion with her for weeks now. Tough or not, Alex knew it was past time he came clean.

Her head turned when he called her name. And his mouth opened to start confessing exactly what was going on with Gwen—but he never had a chance to say it.

She suddenly plopped down those X-rated art books on an antique table in the hall, wheeled straight toward him and yanked his head down to hers.

He'd have been better prepared for a hurricane or a bomb or a fire. Anything but Regan hurling herself in his arms—and a kiss. Granted, he was brain rattled and stressed, but he could have sworn she was hurt. Or angry with him.

Probably she was both, and Alex didn't instantly forget his resolution to talk with her about Gwen. Talking was the wise thing to do. Hell, anything was wiser than hurling himself right back at her. But damnation. She'd owned his hormones from the day he'd met her, and that powerful chemistry was never more than a veil under a thin surface when he was near her.

The hall chandelier glared bald light. The polished parquet floor was hard as rock. There wasn't a chair or soft surface in sight, and the framed pictures of stern-faced ancestors guaranteed no possibility of a romantic atmosphere.

Yet he kissed her back, and tasted magic. The swirl of her tongue, the texture of her silk hair crushed in his fingers, the exotic woman scent of her hit him like two shots of moonshine.

Her hands climbed up his chest, trying to tangle with buttons and push at his shirt at the same time. Her urgency fed his. He dropped his hands to her waist, pushed at her T-shirt, swept around her ribs to the back, snarled with the catch of her bra. She gasped for air; so did he…then came back for another hot, dark kiss involving tongues and teeth and yearning so sharp it clawed at him.

The speed was madness, the place insane, and in two seconds flat, he had no memory of how this forest fire had even started. In the back of his mind, fears pounced—his same-old, same-old, secret fears that he wouldn't please her, that he'd never manage to be that hero she was so afraid to believe in. But the fierce, urgent need pumping through his blood was no simple thing to quell. The yearning in her kisses tasted like the fire of temptation. The longing in her touch burned him from the inside out. He had to have her. It wasn't about sex. It was about the corner of his heart that she owned, would always own, about emotions for her that he'd never had nor could even imagine having for anyone else.

Aw, hell. He wanted her as though he'd die if he couldn't have her. It wasn't any more complicated than that, and when her fingers fumbled at the catch of his jeans, he lost it.

"If you want to say no, Regan," he muttered thickly, "do me a real kindness and say it fast."

"Yes." She tore down the zipper. "Yes." Her smooth warm palm closed over him. "Yes."

He tried for one last scalloped smidgen of sanity. "This isn't the place—"

"You think I give a royal damn where we are? And I'm warning you now, Brennan, if you want to say no—do me a real kindness and say it fast." The way she mimicked his phrasing almost made him smile—but then she kissed him again. "You can forget chivalry for once. I'm on the pill. *Not* because there's been a man in my life for a long time, but I'll explain the why about the pill some other time. I just want you to know that I'm already protected so you can forget it. In fact, forget everything, Alex. Forget the whole damn world but you and me.''

She was on quite a roll with that speech...but she quit talking altogether when he pulled the T-shirt over her head and leveled her against the wall. He had to lift her legs around his waist to get his mouth on her breasts. The silky bra fabric dangled in his eyes. His whiskers rouged her satin-soft skin. Yet her nipples swelled and tightened under the lavish wash of his tongue, and when his teeth nipped at the shadow of her breasts, he could feel her heart thundering, thundering.

She was wearing a skirt, but her legs were bare. Long, supple and bare. There was only a bare scrap of silk between them, and he could feel the moisture on her panties pressing, rubbing against him. ''Let me down,'' she whispered.

''No.''

Frustration hoarsened her voice. ''I can't get them off, Alex, and I want you inside me. Now. And you can't keep holding my weight—''

Oh, yeah, he could. Temporarily he could do damn well anything. They'd shaken hands with chemistry before, but nothing like this. All his life he'd valued honor and pride and being a good man, but no woman had ever made him feel dangerous and wicked before. No woman had ever reached in and touched the core of him the way she did. Her frenzy of frustration seemed to be for him. Her smoking desire seemed to be for him. Her kisses, her touch, expressed painfully naked vulnerability and trust...and somehow, someway, she seemed to feel those things for him.

The silk panties twisted free—or free enough—and he'd rather have kicked off his cumbrous pants, but there wasn't time, not in his head, not in his pounding heart. Squeezing her fanny tight, he found her damp, soft entrance and plunged in like a hot velvet spear seeking its sheath. She groaned a fierce, low hiss of pleasure, and her fingers fisted in his hair, clutching, clutching, her sweet mouth cushioning his as he started a drumming, driving rhythm. Her skin sheened gold. Her eyes closed tight. She cleaved to him until the yearning built like a rage, threatening like lightning before a storm, hot, electric, consuming, spiraling through him until there was nothing else.

She cried out, a wild call, and he felt her body spasming, pulsing in release, first once and then again. Need lashed through him with a powerful whip, yet that was nothing, nothing compared to the emotions bursting loose inside him. Belonging. Rightness. Wonder. Love. When his seed finally spilled, he was breathing louder than a freight train, more spent than if he'd endured a train wreck.

And then it was over. Not instantly. But Alex was suddenly, starkly aware that he'd been pounding into her against a hard stuccoed wall in the baldly lit front hall…and he couldn't hold her weight any longer. His roughness slammed at his conscience with the shock of a baseball bat. He'd never been rough with a woman. It wasn't his nature. And he'd never have willingly risked hurting Regan in a thousand years.

His gaze inhaled her in a single gulp…her tumbled, tousled hair. The red-rouge marks on her breasts from his beard. Neither of them even had their clothes completely off. And the look in her eyes was dazed and dreamy-stunned...maybe fearful?

They both heard a car door slam at the same time.

Merle was home.

And could be turning the key in the front door to the hall any second.

Ten

Regan heard the car door slam. Even with the windows wide open because of the warm night, the sound wasn't loud—just a muffled thud, traveling the long distance from the driveway outside. Still, it snapped her head up as if for the sudden screech of a fire alarm.

One look at Alex's face invoked a far more disastrous mental fire alarm. He was silent, staring into her face. Moments before, he'd let her down, so they were both standing upright, but one of his hands had lifted to her hair, was idly caressing a strand near her cheek. And damnation, his eyes were intensely focused, absorbed. He had incredibly emotive eyes. Sexy eyes. Eyes that could hypnotize a woman without half trying.

It would be nice to wallow in that look in his eyes— next year. She wasn't positive he realized his brother was back home. Hell's bells, when Alex really got concentrating, she wasn't positive he'd notice if a troop of Marines had arrived on the front porch.

"Alex!" Her voice was a hiss. A single-word scold was the best she could manage. She yanked her skirt down. Yanked his flapping shirt closed over that fascinatingly hairy chest. Yanked frantically behind her to reclasp the hooks on her bra.

That was a lot of yanking to pull off simultaneously. Accidentally her head rammed into his nose. Accidentally her elbow crashed into his ribs. She stepped on his feet, which couldn't have hurt him too much—she was barefoot—but because Alex instinctively shot a hand to his injured nose, then to his injured ribs, somehow he wasn't getting his jeans pulled up, much less zipped.

She heard Merle turning the key in the front door lock. Frantically her gaze flew around the hall, searching for her T-shirt—and she saw it lying in a puddle on the parquet floor, but it was too far away to risk the time retrieving it then. She grabbed Alex's arm and hustled them both inside the nearest doorway.

Out of breath, she latched the library door, at least ensuring them a couple minutes of privacy. But she'd barely whirled around before Alex calmly, quietly hooked his fingers around both her wrists.

"Are we feeling, um, just a little shook-up?"

"You didn't hear your brother coming in?"

"I heard him. But I was distracted for a few seconds, thinking you might just have broken my nose trying to rescue us." He'd managed the zip on his jeans by then, if not the button, and there was laughter in his eyes...but a lot more than laughter. His whole expression reflected the potent, raw, intimate memory of what they'd been doing only moments before.

Color heated her cheeks. She'd had to move fast, with

the threat of Merle discovering them…but her awkward
bumbling and fumbling certainly annihilated any hint of
an intimate mood. And what had been an irrevocably
soul-touching experience—like nothing she'd ever
dreamed of—suddenly became wrong. Crazy wrong.
Mortifyingly all wrong. She could so easily picture her
incurably romantic Alex in a seductive setting with cham-
pagne and soft words and some polite moonlit darkness.
Not in a front hall. Clothes half ripped off. Standing up.
Under the glaring light of a chandelier.

A lump clogged Regan's throat. She still wasn't sure
what had gotten into her. She remembered being rattled
over Gwen. And Regan knew perfectly well she was nobody's princess—and certainly not Alex's vision of a perfect, ideal woman. But that Pastel Paragon was so obviously trying to sink her hooks back in Alex, and
somehow it had seemed terribly important to make sure
he knew there were alternatives. Not perfect alternatives,
not *ideal* alternatives, but flesh-and-blood real women
who could care about him.

Like her, for instance.

She understood all that. It was how a justifiably impulsive hug had turned into a tidal wave that confounded
her. Heaven knew, hormones were wily beasts, but she'd
never experienced or expected that wanton, lusty, abandoned response he'd aroused in her. And Alex…holy kamoly. His hair was standing up in rumpled thatches; she
saw a scratch mark on his throat; and some disgracefully
brazen woman had put a hickey on his neck where it
showed.

She shook her head. "You look wasted," she announced, and suddenly in spite of everything, grinned.
"Good."

"Good?"

"Yeah. You are. Incredibly good, Brennan." She was charmed, watching a flush climb up his neck. But not surprised to see the sudden guilt clouding his eyes.

"Um, Regan...did we attend the same event? The words *fast, rough* and *insensitive* come to mind. I can't even give you an excuse for losing my head—"

"Don't make me regret this by saying you're sorry," she said fiercely.

He caught her hand, clasped it. Outside in the hall she could hear the clip of footsteps, and there wasn't a scrap of material in the whole darn library to cover herself with—nor did she know where her shoes were. If Alex heard his brother, he gave no sign. He just looked at her with those mesmerizing blue eyes.

"I don't want you to regret this," he said quietly, gently. "But there are things we should have talked about. Before making love—"

"Like protection, and you have to be wondering why I was on the pill." She swallowed hard. She'd never been less than honest with him, and couldn't be now. "I saw a doc a couple of weeks ago when I realized this could happen. Not because I planned on sleeping with you, Alex, I swear. To be frank, I thought the opposite—that we never would. But I don't take chances with babies, and I'm just too old to pretend to myself that the risk wasn't there. I—"

"The last thing on my mind was why you were on the pill." He was still threading his fingers with hers, his hands big, warm, dry. Hers were darn near dripping with nerves.

"Then Gwen. You think we should have talked about Gwen first...." She heard Merle's voice calling both of them from behind the closed door. And still, Alex looked at no one but her. "But you're not engaged to her now.

There's nothing for you to feel guilty about. And I didn't pretend to myself about that, either. I was aware you had feelings for Gwen—''

"No. You *don't* know what my feelings for Gwen are, and that's exactly what I should have told you before this or anything else happened.''

"You don't owe me any explanation.'' Again she heard Merle's voice calling. She still had nothing on above the waist but a bra. "Alex, I *have* to go—''

"Not yet.''

"Just stop worrying about this, all right? I'm an adult woman, and I take my own risks. As far as I'm concerned, this wasn't about her or anyone else in any way. It was just about you and me.''

"I agree with that. A thousand percent. No one, Regan, was on my mind but you.'' He finally released her hands, but only to touch her cheek, the caress as soft and poignant as a whisper. "But I need to talk with you. I want to explain—''

Merle's voice loomed closer. Too close. Trauma was piling on top of trauma—his incredible lovemaking was one thing, but everything since had turned disastrous. Not that she'd allowed herself to believe in the fairy tale, but just once in her life—with him—she'd desperately wanted something to go right. Instead, she'd almost given him a black eye, bruised his ribs, inelegantly chased him into a hiding place, and somehow post-loving cuddling had turned into a discussion about another woman. Life could always get worse, but the thought of Merle barging in and finding her half-dressed was definitely not something she was prepared to face at that moment.

She bolted for the open French doors. "I understand you want to talk. But not now. Later, okay? I'll call you tomorrow or the next day—''

"Now wait, just wait..." But she'd already crossed the threshold when she suddenly heard the tone of his voice completely change. "Regan? Holy Henry. You're not wearing any top!"

Oh, God. She almost laughed as she raced across the dew-soaked grass, jogging the circumference of the house toward the front driveway. Her bare feet were coated with grass by the time she climbed into her car, and she was shivering badly from the chilled night air. No shoes, no shirt, no purse—if she hadn't left her car keys in the ignition, she'd be stranded without those, too.

She started the engine, thinking that if a cop stopped her, she'd have a lot to explain.

But a cop she could handle. If Alex had managed to stop her from leaving, she doubted her ability to handle any of the "explanations" he had in mind.

She didn't want to hear his regrets. She didn't want to hear him gently, chivalrously, tactfully avoid hurting her with a direct rejection. For sure she didn't want to hear one more blasted word about the blond princess...but as she zoomed home, his ex-fiancée was a cringing thought that clawed at her heart.

The kind of woman who belonged in the Brennan mansion would never be driving in a bra and bare feet. She'd never nearly break her lover's nose two seconds after making love. And she'd be a nice woman. A good woman. A woman with some dignity. The kind of woman who didn't lose her head with her guy in semi-public places.

Regan pulled into her driveway, checked to make sure no neighbors were wandering the sidewalks and then pelted for her back door. Abruptly she stopped dead. Naturally, with her purse still at Alex's house, she had no house key. Aw, hell. Somehow she was going to have to break in.

She squeezed her eyes closed just for a second, willing back tears. Tears were stupid. Where was her sense of humor? She'd always been able to laugh at herself on those days that turned into a comedy of errors.

But she just couldn't seem to laugh tonight. She'd never wanted to play a comedy role in Alex's life. And everything that had gone wrong seemed to illustrate in block letters how totally wrong she was for him.

Finding a way into her house presented no real challenge. Eventually she discovered a loose screen on a window and heaved herself up and in. But finding a way to control her feelings for Alex was a challenge she had no answers for. She'd been in love before—but never this hard, never this deeply, never as if she was missing part of herself when they were apart.

For years Regan had been so careful not to sell herself the fairy tale again. The irony didn't escape her. She'd found a good man—a man she valued and fiercely loved far more than any damn stupid hero. Only the happy-ending part of the story still broke down...because she simply couldn't be the damsel he was looking for.

Alex had just stepped out of the shower and hooked a towel around his waist when his brother rapped on the bathroom door. Merle poked his head in.

"I wondered where you'd disappeared to. It was suddenly so quiet around here. When I first got home, I could have sworn I saw Regan's car still in the drive."

Alex grabbed a second towel to dry his hair. "It was. But Regan never planned to stay late. There's less than two weeks left in the school term for her, and she had a ton of work to do."

"Uh-huh. For the record, I got Gwen home okay."

"Thanks," Alex said shortly.

"Far as I could tell, there was nothing wrong with her car. I'd guess she trumped up that excuse so she could contrive some time with you."

Alex had suspected the same thing, but the problem of Gwen was nothing he was willing to discuss with his brother—nor was she remotely on his mind at the moment. Merle, however, seemed inclined to stay parked in the doorway, oblivious to the clouds of humid steam wafting past him.

"Did, um, you and Regan happen to do anything interesting after I left?"

Alex abruptly quit rubbing his wet head and yanked off the towel to take a studying look at his brother's face. "Sure. We talked."

"Uh-huh. I figured that."

"You figured exactly *what*, bro?"

Merle's expression was beneficently innocent. "I figured your conversation must have been pretty interesting, because Regan seemed to have lost a few things." He stepped into the bathroom and piled a T-shirt, sandals and a purse on the counter next to Alex. "I'm hoping you won't make the same mistake."

"The same mistake?" Alex echoed blankly.

"Yeah. You tend to be forgetful, too...but in your shoes, I'd be real careful not to lose *her*."

Merle closed the door on that exit line, saving Alex having to respond. He wiped the mirror clear of steam and hung up the towels, but his gaze kept straying to the skimpy sandals, the soft-fabric T-shirt, the suitcase-sized tote Regan called a purse.

Regan had managed to win the respect of his stubbornly misogynist brother—surprising Alex not at all.

But par for the course, his brother's interfering advice was worth buckshot.

Alex didn't have Regan to lose. Never had.

Scooping up her things, he padded barefoot across the hall and closed the door on his bedroom. Without turning on a light, he dropped her things on his bed, then stalked over to the open balcony doors stark-naked, the cool moonlight raising gooseflesh on his skin—not really from chill, more from ominous nerves.

The Replay button refused to quit in his head, of their wild coming together, taking her against a wall for Pete's sake, nothing in his mind but heat. Heat for her. Heat with her. A fire so out of control he'd been burning for her from the inside out.

Still was.

He washed a hand over his face, thinking that he'd done nothing right with Regan from the day he met her. Corny or not, he believed in wooing a woman. He believed in the courtship rituals—flowers, moonlight, romancing, dancing, the whole shebang—believed that a woman deserved all those attentions and symbols of respect and appreciation. He'd never wooed Regan. Hell. He was dead positive she'd screech at him in a feminist harangue if he even tried.

But making love with her like an animal in heat—especially the first time—pushed all his guilt buttons. Memories pounced in his mind. He'd spilled embarrassing truths before he ever knew her, came on to her in the front seat of a car like a schoolboy, bungled the evening at the beach, bungled explaining about Gwen. Hell, he'd bungled everything.

But if he'd been remotely alive before knowing Regan, he didn't think so. Sunshine was exciting when he was with her. The air he breathed had more oxygen. Everything in his life was sharper, different—God knew, not easier—but rocket-packed with vibrance. Joy of life. Joy of being.

Deliberately Alex touched the tender bump near his eye. He'd be lucky if it wasn't a shiner by tomorrow, and that wasn't the first time Regan had given him a blunt, inelegant whomp upside the head. For weeks now, her suggestion that he'd understood love as an ideal instead of the real thing had ticked him off.

But the damn woman he loved was right. For a long time he'd believed what he felt for Gwen was the most ideal kind of love. Being with Regan, from the first moment, had been the punch of a different kind of reality. Gwen had never stirred him to a lust attack, much less inspired him to daydream about orgies. The ideal love he'd sought with Gwen seemed tepid by comparison to any and all emotions Regan inspired with him—even when they were arguing up a storm.

Alex squeezed his eyes closed. He should have told her weeks ago that he had no lingering feelings for Gwen. Maybe he'd been petrified that a quiet, gentlemanly type of guy could never satisfy her for long. Hell, who was he kidding? He was still petrified.

But there was no way he could make love with Regan and just let it go. An uncommitted affair was not his way—nor was it hers. Sex changed the stakes. Making love had not only complicated her vulnerability. It upped his fear—and his risk of failing her.

Believing he could convince a woman who'd lost her trust in men—and love—to take a chance on him defied all logical reason. And Alex was glumly, grimly aware that he was running out of time. They'd easily, naturally run into each other over the school year, but those opportunities would disappear like smoke during the sum-

mer. She could easily elude him. Move on. Regan had a
history of disappearing from men who'd hurt her before.

He could either win her. Or lose her. But Alex could
hear the ominously ticking clock in his heart. Whatever
happened—whatever he did—had to be soon.

Regan jogged up the library steps, breathless and juggling an armload of papers and books. She pushed open
the door with her hair flying in her face.

Mrs. McGurty glanced up from the front desk. "Why,
honey, you're really running late tonight. I don't know
if you realized the time, but I'll be closing up here within
a half hour—"

"I know, I know. But I don't need to bother you to
check out anything—just a couple minutes to look up
something and I'll be gone."

"Well, I like that new brown hair color, dear. Kind
of...chestnutty. Of course I liked the red you had before
this, but I don't know, this one's such a nice, warm, rich
brown I think I like it even better."

"Thanks, Mrs. McGurty—" The librarian was a
sweetie, but she was slightly prone to talk all night. Regan hustled past and ducked down the aisle she wanted.
This close to nine, there wasn't another soul in the place,
and she started whistling under her breath. Maybe she
was a little harried right now, but overall life was going
hunky-dory.

In fact, life had been going hunky-dory for the entire
last week—which was the last thing Regan had expected
after that never-to-be-mentioned-again night with Alex.

She crouched down, skimming titles, plucking books
to add to the stack in her arms, musing that nothing could
possibly have gone better. Alex had shown up the next
morning with her purse and things—but he'd also

brought a box of raspberry sugared doughnuts. They'd pigged out and laughed, and he'd never mentioned the previous night.

He'd done a few bewildering things since, she mentally acknowledged. The night she'd had the girls over for poker, a delivery truck had suddenly arrived, bearing ten pounds of Godiva chocolates. Ten pounds, wrapped in gold, better than sin...hell's bells, the dark chocolates were—almost—better than sex. Which was not precisely how she expressed a thank-you to Alex, but he'd just chuckled and claimed she'd mentioned her addiction to chocolate sometime and he just thought she'd like them.

She had. The next day she'd found two huge, fragrant, extravagant pots of gardenias waiting on her porch steps when she'd come home from school. For an instant she'd been panic-stricken. Had someone died? Had he lost his mind? Why on earth would he be sending her such a thing? But when she'd called, inquiring about his mental health, he'd just calmly said that he figured the end of the school year was frazzling and maybe she needed a pick-me-up.

She had. A couple of days after that, a delivery truck bearing live lobsters from Maine had shown up at her door...and so had Alex, minutes later. He'd cooked the suckers himself—there couldn't possibly have been a messier, butter-dripping dinner—and they'd laughed and watched a movie later, slouched on the couch with the kittens.

Regan was a little uneasy with those strange gifts...but he hadn't made a pass. There had been no passes, no mention of Gwen, and not even the teensiest reference to that One Night. She was thrilled, she told herself grimly. Downright ecstatic. Beside-herself happy.

And if lying to herself didn't work, she'd try something else. She refused to stop seeing Alex. No matter what the risk to her heart, she was still worried that he was under Gwen's spell, still felt honor bound as a friend to protect him from hurt if she could. Loving him meant more than just thinking about herself.

Abruptly she glanced at the books at her feet. Somehow while her mind had strayed to Alex, the two research tomes she'd wanted to look up mysteriously turned into seven. This wasn't the first time she'd noticed the phenomenon. Unsupervised books—like rabbits—showed a disastrous amoral tendency to reproduce.

The clock was still ticking. Knowing she only had a few minutes before the library closed, she hurriedly started heaping—purse, papers, file folders, books, then more books. When she stood up, the whole load tried to stagger and shift...so she ran pell-mell for the back table behind the myths and legends aisle.

She was so positive the library was deserted that finding anyone was a surprise—but spotting Alex at "their" table was a special electric jolt on her nerves. At that instant she had no time to dwell on it or even to say hi. One book crashed to the floor. Then another toppled. Papers flew. Those spilling out of her hands hit the table in a small tidal wave.

Alex was already on his feet, chuckling and playing police for all the escaping debris. "I'll be darned. Didn't we play out this exact same scene before?" he asked dryly.

She laughed. "Yes, you rat. I swear you have a gift for catching me at my worst. I was just in such a hurry—I knew there were only a few minutes before the library closed, and there were just a couple things I really wanted to look up tonight."

"Well, I landed here because I wanted a quiet place

to grade exams, and Merle had people over at the house...but I'm about done." He glanced at her books. "You're doing some kind of research on Margaret Mitchell, *Gone with the Wind?*"

"Yeah. It's for a seminar I'm doing over the summer. 'Contemporary Heroes Gone Wrong.' Starting with Ashley Wilkes..." Nerves pooled in her stomach just to look at him. Her fingers metamorphosed into thumbs. He was just wearing casual Dockers and a T-shirt, but making love with him had changed everything. She knew intimately what the chest hair under that shirt felt like. She knew precisely what that beard could do to her tender skin. She knew exactly how much trouble that mouth could inspire.

Since that thought train was disastrous, she spilled out a steady stream of light chatter. "You remember Ashley. Scarlett's secret heartthrob in the story. His heroic behavior created a mess if ever there was one. It would have been simple enough for him to tell Scarlett to take a hike, move it along, grow up, get over it, girl. But no. That wasn't heroic behavior on Ashley's terms. He had to be nice. He had to be polite and chivalrous, because those were the ideals he lived by. And because he couldn't forget those damn ideals, Scarlett's attraction for him was allowed to fester and grow—"

She was just warming up when Alex interrupted her. "I think I've heard this part before," he said wryly.

"You couldn't have. I just started working on this seminar about Ashley."

"I understand that, but the last time we talked, you were researching some fairy tale—'The Emperor's New Clothes'? The story about this poor guy running around, desperate to wear those imaginary fancy clothes, because he didn't think he was cool enough as he was. As you described it, he was scared he wasn't hero enough. That he wasn't a man enough to be anyone's ideal—''

"Yes, yes." She nodded vigorously. "That theme is just everywhere. Men who think they have to be heroes. Who think they have to fit some *ideal* standard instead of just being themselves—"

"Uh-huh. And before that, you were exuberantly going on about another fairy tale. What was it?… I remember, 'The Nightingale.' Where the guy captures this songbird and puts it in a cage—only because he wanted to treasure it—but as he discovered, the bird stopped singing when it was locked up. You can't cage an ideal. Regan?''

"What?" She caught the sudden, strange gleam in his eyes, the odd tension in his jaw. But this whole subject made her happy. If he didn't want to talk about Gwen, he certainly didn't have to. But she thought she could keep doing this sneakily. Help him. Engrain the thought in his head that a real woman wouldn't expect or want him to be an ideal. That his feelings for Gwen could well have been an ideal of love instead of the real thing.

He leaned forward. "I've had it with the lectures. I'm out of patience—and you just ran out of time, Regan. You'd better brace yourself, because you're in real trouble with me—and I'm not kidding.''

"Trouble?" The expression in his eyes made her breath catch. She'd never seen him look furious before— certainly not at her—and she really had no idea what he was talking about.

At that precise moment, though, Mrs. McGurty bustled around the corner, tch-tching and wagging her finger when she spotted them. "Honestly, you two. I almost locked up without checking to be sure you were gone. It's several minutes past closing time now—"

"We're sorry," they both told her. Regan didn't look

at Alex, but he stood up as quickly as she did to start gathering up their debris.

"I've got a couple more things to do in the back room, but I'm telling you, I'm locking the front doors no later than five minutes from now," Mrs. McGurty warned them.

"We'll be out of here in two," Alex assured her. "In fact, we're headed for the door right now."

"Okeydoke, dears. I probably won't hear when you leave, so I'll just say good-night now, and we'll see you soon." Mrs. McGurty smiled at them and then disappeared.

Nervously Regan pushed a strand of hair from her temple, glancing uneasily at Alex and then at her stack of books. "I need to put these back on the shelves before I go."

Alex, his head down, was already grabbing some of the heavier tomes from her pile. "I'll help you put them back. Just show me where they go."

His voice sounded even and calm again, but her nerves were still shredding. "Alex, what did you mean? That I was in trouble? Are you angry with me about something?"

Eleven

Alex took off, carrying an armload of her books. Fretfully Regan raked a hand through her hair. He hadn't answered her. Obviously they both needed to hustle to put the books back with the library imminently closing. Logically they could talk any old time. Right now they were both in a hurry.

Only her heart was beating in big, thick thuds. She was in trouble with him? They argued all the time, had from the first, but she'd always thought he loved those debates. She didn't know of anything she could have done to offend Alex, and she hurt from the inside out at the thought that she may have.

"Alex..." She scooped up the rest of her research books and sprinted after him. He wasn't hard to find. He was already hunkered down, threading a book in its appropriate spot on the bottom shelf. She hunkered down, too. "*Are* you angry with me?" she repeated.

"Yes."

Yes? What kind of answer was that? She tried to search his face, but he bounced to his feet, reading the numbers of the book spines to find the right spot for another tome.

She bounced to her feet, too. "Are we talking a little angry or a lot angry?" she asked delicately.

"We're talking as ticked off as I can ever remember being with a woman." He snapped a book in place just so, then carted another book three feet down to the end of the aisle.

She galloped those three feet after him, feeling a lump in her throat heavier than lead. "Brennan, it wouldn't kill you to be a little more forthcoming. I don't know what I said to make you mad. Could you at least give me a clue?"

"You want a clue? I'll give you a crystal-clear clue," he said, and spun around.

He grabbed her by the shoulders faster than she could gulp a breath, and suddenly his mouth was there, taking hers, claiming hers, like some ravaging pirate staking his claim on stolen treasure. The books slipped out of her hands. Her purse dropped and spilled. It was a terrible mistake to reward such appalling macho behavior, but damn.

No one could kiss like him. No one. Her eyes closed, and her arms wound around his waist. She felt his tense muscles and the heat pouring off his skin, sensing Alex was out of control for the first time since she'd known him. She tasted need, like hellfire. She tasted tenderness, like desperation. She tasted the man she loved, inhaling every texture and scent and sound that identified him so uniquely as her Alex.

Lights flickered on, then off. Footsteps clipped past—

undoubtedly Mrs. McGurty, dutifully checking one last time to make sure they were gone. But they'd both picked up all their belongings from the back table, so the librarian had no reason to suspect they were still around. The sound of her clip-cloppy heels faded. Then the library lights winked off for good. It wasn't true dark…more dusky, with the pearled, jeweled hues of sunset reflecting in the distant library windows. The place was suddenly silent. So silent that all she could hear was his husky breathing and the rapid pounding of her own heart.

"Alex…?" He let her up for air—long enough to inhale a lungful of oxygen, then his lips were trailing a hot, slow, wet trail down her throat. And his hands… For once she was wearing a relatively demure green top with shorts. His fingers were steadily inching that top up, and in one flick, he'd conquered the front clasp of her bra.

"Alex…" she repeated, trying to say his name more firmly. But just at that moment the top was skimming over her head. She was unsure if he heard her. She was less sure if he cared. She'd noticed before that Alex had that tiny personality flaw. He wasn't absentminded, but he was a terribly dangerous man when his concentration was singularly directed. Still, one of them needed to be the designated realist. "Alex? I'm afraid we may already be locked in."

"I don't give a royal damn." The instant the T-shirt cleared the top of her head, he hurled the scrap of cloth. "You don't, either." He took her mouth again, in a deep, dark, dizzying kiss that had some terrifying effect on her sense of gravity. She knew for sure they were both standing up when it started, but somehow it didn't finish until her shorts had disappeared, several books had cascaded from a shelf and she was twisted beneath him on the rough, gray carpet. "I don't want to hear any more sneaky little lectures about men who goof up being heroes."

"Okay, okay." To hell with being the designated realist. She drank in another kiss, well aware there were prices to pay when a woman skydived without a parachute. She didn't care. She never seemed to care about anything when she was with Alex—but him. Being with him. Being part of him.

"I don't want to hear any more lectures about men who've screwed up, confused some ideal of love instead of valuing the real thing."

"I swear. You won't."

"I got the message. I got it a long time ago, Regan. And maybe I'll fail you. That was always the thing—that I didn't want to be another man in your life who turned out to have feet of clay. Damn it. I'd be a hero for you if I could—"

His muttering lacked a certain coherence, murmured between slow, molasses-slow, bites he was taking out of her neck, her throat, her shoulder. She managed to catch her breath, but somehow her voice came out thready and hoarse. "How many times do I have to tell you? I never wanted a hero."

"The hell you don't. We all want that. Someone who'll be there when the chips are down. Someone who'll spin magic in our world and make you crazy and scare you, really scare you, with how deep and huge those feelings are."

"Alex..." It really was increasingly hard to get a word in. "You're scaring me."

"Good," he murmured. "But let's just see if we can scare you a whole lot more than this."

She wanted to raise a hand and take a time-out to discuss that program, but both her hands were around him just then. Touching him seemed more important. More important than food, water, shelter or anything else on that inconsequential survival list.

His shirt had to go. His pants. Her cheek nuzzled against the whorled hair on his chest; her leg nuzzled between his. Her hands, she discovered, were trembling. It wasn't the first time Alex had had this effect on her. The headlights of a passing car winked in the windows. The dusk slowly turned into midnight black, magic black. The smell of books and the silky darkness were all part of the spell...but the real spell taking her under had his name on it.

The other night they'd come together in a frenzy. This was more a slow race to madness. She could feel a complete, frightening yielding from deep inside her, compelled by the terrible vulnerability she felt with him. She wanted him, wanted this. No one had ever made her feel like the woman she wanted to be. Only him. There was no hiding anything with Alex, never had been, maybe never could be.

She couldn't help loving him. No matter what the emotional price, this felt so right. Kisses heated. Flesh turned hot, damp, slick. He trailed kisses from her temple to her toes, then retraced the same slow, languid path...only, he seemed to get lost halfway. His tongue took a side road on her inner thigh, then dipped down for a kiss so intimate that she bucked toward him like a helpless wave caught in a relentless tide. "Alex...stop. I can't take any more of this."

"Sure you can." Momentarily he lifted his head, but she barely caught the shadow of an unholy grin. "So you're a natural blond, Ms. Stuart. Who'd ever have known?'' He made her almost laugh, when she was in no mood to laugh at all.

"Don't tease. Not anymore. Come to me—"

"We rushed the other night. I'll be damned if we're rushing anything this time. I'm sorry, love, but you're just not going to get your way on this, so resign yourself."

Maybe it was his calling her "love." Maybe it was feeling the love in his touch, in his voice. But she suddenly remembered his confessing that he was afraid of failing her. Alex had always had a number of things terribly goofed up. Always, she'd been the one afraid of failing him, and never more than now. She was nobody's princess, but with Alex she could never seem to be more than frail, and nakedly, vulnerably human.

And there was retribution to pay for making her this afraid. She twisted around, frustrated by the narrow aisle between bookshelves, aggravated by the darkness and purse straps that tried to tangle with her feet. But she managed to take her turn at that marathon kissing. Her resolve was unbending. She wanted the blood rushing through his veins until he couldn't think, wanted need clawing through him until he couldn't breathe, wanted his whole world electrified...the way he'd electrified hers. Possibly no one had ever kissed his belly button. The back of his knees. Unquestionably, though, a stroking kiss on a particular part of his anatomy inspired a volatilely physical response. She wasn't sure she was doing anything right...but it seemed, it *really* seemed that driving him out of his mind was a reachable goal.

She was still testing that possibility when he scooped her onto her back again. Dark eyes loomed over her. Silvery light made his bones look tense and taut, chiseled sharp with desire. "We're all done playing," he warned her.

It was the first time Alex had ever lied to her. He wasn't done playing at all.... The first time he claimed her body with the tenderness of a knight with a virgin damsel; the next time he was a kidnapping pirate intent on wicked ravishment. The next time he was a prince courting his princess. They were in a library, probably locked in, their mattress a scratchy, gray carpet, and the hours kept passing. He either didn't know or completely didn't care. He whispered the fantasies to her, all the fantasies, all the silly foolish fantasies that she was too smart—too scared—to believe in. But this wasn't about believing that frogs turned into princes. It was about trusting Alex, with that secret, private corner of her heart, feeling safe with him, safe enough to play, safe enough to let her heart soar and her inhibitions fly away because everything with him was right. Loving him made it right.

Later—heaven knew how late—she crashed on his chest more tired than a whipped puppy. "Brennan," she whispered, "I don't want to embarrass you by using that word *hero*, but you could darn well give lessons in legendary prowess."

"Maybe I just had some legendary inspiration." He smoothed her hair, cuddling her close. "Regan?"

"Hmm?"

"I love you."

Her heart seemed to forget how to beat. An instant before, she'd been tired enough to sleep through a hurricane. Now she lifted her head and stared into his eyes, unsure if she'd imagined him saying those words, scared to believe he really meant them.

"No," he murmured. He stroked her hair again, touched her cheek. "We're not going to talk about this now. I think both of us need some serious sleep, and temporarily we have a small, critical problem that really won't wait any longer to be solved.''

Those three fearsome, wondrous words were still making her heart spin...but she had to smile. ''You don't like the idea of someone opening up the library doors in the morning and finding us sleeping naked on the floor?''

''I'd just as soon no one saw you in this condition, Ms. Stuart, but me. On the other hand, how to break out of this place without setting off an alarm system and getting ourselves arrested may just be a tad tricky.''

''Well, it burns me to say this...you can't imagine how much...but this does seem to be a problem that calls for a hero. Have you got a plan to rescue me, sir?''

''*Now* you want me to be a hero? Whatever happened to the fair damsel taking charge and rescuing her guy?''

Alex got her laughing...but that moment seemed to start a chain of disasters. In principle, he was used to that. Nothing he'd ever wanted to do with Regan had gone right. She had a gift for catching him at his worst, but this was a time when he needed—seriously, badly, desperately needed—to be at his best.

Breaking out of the library wasn't that challenging. He discovered the doors were wired with an alarm system and padlocked from the outside, and by the time Regan was dressed, he'd found an old casement window on the main floor that was easily breachable. Regan was still chortling laughter when they leapt to the ground and dusted themselves off—but that was the last thing that went well.

Once outside, she spotted both their cars in the parking lot, and her whole mood seemed to change. Her moonlit face suddenly radiated a painful, vulnerable unsureness when she hesitantly suggested that she'd better leave him and drive home. She had work tomorrow. She had cats. She'd be stuck with a car to pick up later unless she drove her own now.

Alex knew she was hopelessly attached to the hellions, but the cats had been fed—he'd asked—and he sensed the rest were just excuses. He understood it would be a pain in the keester to pick up her car later. He understood she was exhausted. He understood she needed sleep. He understood, even more, that his words of love had shaken her up.

Hell, he was just as shaken. The floor of the public library was no place to blurt out his heart. One of many damn fool moves he'd made with her, but he had no intention of willingly separating from Regan—not for hours, not even for minutes—until they had a private place and the right time to seriously talk.

So he conned her into going home with him, and possibly because she was so dizzy tired, she didn't argue that hard. For a short time he built up brash hopes that he could make this come out right. Her exhaustion was working in his favor. At his place, he tiptoed with her up the back stairs to his wing, stripped her down and poured her into his monster-sized antique bed. She hurled herself into his arms like a snuggling kitten, reassuring him that maybe, just maybe, she wasn't going to reject him. If they could both just catch some rest, he'd have another chance to recoup from his blurting and bumbling and say everything right, do everything right. And just before she dozed off, she murmured a sweet, soft sound. A loving sound.

The next sound he heard—less than an hour later—was the trumpeting screech of an alarm clock. He bolted out of bed and slapped the thing off. Regan opened her eyes. "No," he whispered. "Go back to sleep. I'll call both our schools. It won't kill either of us to play hookey one day out of the year.... I'll be right back, love, I promise."

Bleary-eyed, he stumbled into the upstairs office and called her school, then his school. He hadn't missed a day in two years—and doubted she had, either—but damned if anything or anyone was going to intrude until he had some time alone with her. He climbed back into bed and spooned protectively around her, closing his eyes when she nuzzled her head against his shoulder.

Minutes later, the echo of clomping footsteps barged into his consciousness, and suddenly there was Merle's face, poking in the doorway. "Hell, Alex, I thought you must be sick when you didn't come down for breakfas— Oh. *Oh.* Well, I'll be damned...."

Alex had already covered Regan's head with a sheet. He viewed his brother's unholy grin with a scowl. "Out."

"Why, sure, bro. Good morning, Regan."

"Good morning, Merle," murmured a sleepy, muffled voice.

"I'm delighted, more delighted than you can imagine, to see you with us—"

"*Out,* Merle."

"Okay, okay..."

Once Merle disappeared, nothing more could go wrong. Alex was sure. They just needed a few hours' solid rest, and Regan readily dropped off again. So did he. Yet it seemed only a few minutes passed before his eyelids snapped wide open again. A voice interrupted his sleep this time. A feminine voice he recognized all too well, trilling "Hello, anyone home?" from the base of the stairs.

Alex tried convincing himself that this was a nightmare. Everyone tended to have bad dreams when they were extrastressed. No matter how often or how badly he'd bungled romantic moments with Regan before, this morning was absolutely critical with her. Terrifyingly critical. Fate would never be so unkind as to add his ex-fiancée to the equation. Never.

Gwen's soprano trilled out another cheerful "Hello?"

Alex dove out of bed and yanked on his jeans with the speed of despair—but not so fast he didn't see Regan stirring. "No, no," he said soothingly. "Go back to sleep. Just forget you heard anything. I'll take care of it and be right back."

The words were barely out of his mouth before he realized it was no good. Regan had obviously recognized the voice, too. She groggily leaned up on an elbow, her face still soft and vulnerable with sleep, but those huge, shadowed eyes of hers were wide-awake. Too awake.

"Regan, I swear this is not what you think. There are a hundred things I want to tell you. That I wish I'd told you last night. But if you'd just try and trust me for a few minutes—"

"Alex," she said gently, "calm down. If you're assuming I was going to leap to conclusions—"

Hell, yes, he assumed she was leaping to conclusions, and for damn sure there was no prayer of his calming down. Still snapping his jeans, he left the room and jogged for the stairs. Halfway down, he saw Merle hustling from the kitchen carrying a spatula—and belatedly realized Regan was just behind him, wrapping his oversize robe around her. Both of them spotted Gwen. Hell, so did he.

"Alex, I didn't think you'd be home on a weekday morning, but I saw your car in the drive and I...oh, dear." Gwen's pretty blue eyes zoomed past his head to the sight of Regan at the top of the stairs, barefoot and still knotting the sash on his robe. She sucked in a delicate breath. "I can see I should have called before coming. But it was ten in the morning. It never occurred to me—"

"Uh-huh." When Alex reached the bottom of the stairs, he politely hooked Gwen's arm and just as politely yanked her into the living room. He caught a glimpse of Regan's eyes just before he slammed the doors closed, but, tarnation. He knew how this was going to go—how it *had* to go. And it was nothing he wanted Regan exposed to if he could help it.

When he pivoted around, Gwen lifted a hand in a conciliatory gesture. "Alex, I apologize. I didn't realize you had anyone else here."

"Maybe you didn't. But this is the third time you've pulled this since you came back home." Regan didn't know that, but it was one of the hundred things Alex wanted to tell her—that she positively didn't need to worry about Gwen because he'd already talked to his ex-fiancée. Which he had. Only it was mortifyingly, glaringly apparent to him now that his previous efforts to kindly, tactfully suggest she take a powder were like getting through to bedrock.

"You're angry with me," she said hesitantly.

"No. Absolutely not angry at all, Gwen. The truth is, when you took off with Lance, you saved me an incredible amount of heartache—for which I'm grateful and always will be."

"Saved you...?"

He didn't offer her a chair. Didn't budge from the door. "I'd like to think we shared something good. I'd even call that feeling a kind of love. But it's obvious to me now that you saw me as some kind of mentor or father figure. Security. Someone to take care of you. Nothing wrong with that, but it would never have made you happy for long—and it's the same for me. I didn't know what I was missing until I met Regan...and then I discovered I was missing absolutely everything that mattered in my life. I wish you well. I sincerely mean that.''

When he put his hand on the doorknob, she said swiftly, ''If we could just talk about this—''

''We just did. If you have to hear it bluntly, there's only one woman who belongs in my house and my life— and that's Regan. You're leaving. And I do mean right now.''

When he yanked open the doors, Merle was miraculously waiting just outside, holding Gwen's jacket. All Alex saw was that Regan was nowhere in sight. With his heart clanging alarm bells, he took the stairs up two at a time. He found Regan in his bedroom, but increasing his feelings of panic, she'd already pulled on her shorts and was burrowing into her T-shirt.

He walked in, closed the door and latched it, then jogged over to unplug the phone. When he spun around, she'd pulled the shirt over her head and her face had emerged. Her hair looked like tousled silk, her face more pale than pearls in the iridescent morning sunlight. It was the huge, haunting eyes that touched his heart, though, no differently than they had the first day he met her.

''Were you planning on locking me in?'' she asked.

''It was either lock you in or have a heart attack. I need to talk with you. *Alone*. I had in mind both of us getting sleep first—and I sure didn't plan on my ex-fiancée showing up—but I can't risk any more hell breaking loose. Please listen to me, Regan.''

''I'm listening, but I can see you're all upset.'' She

patted the spot on the bed next to her. "Maybe if you sit down, you can try and calm down."

He didn't want to sit. Couldn't sit. He paced around the circumference of the bed, stubbing his bare foot on the bedpost once, clawing a hand through his hair, the words coming out in a jumbled tumble.

"First, I want to get the subject of Gwen over and done with. I handled that situation worse than a kid in grade school. I should have taken a lesson from you. You're terrific with being blunt and honest—but no, I was trying to be kind and not deliberately humiliate her. That didn't work. I can see now, nothing less than a sledgehammer was going to work—"

"Alex, you're going to wear a hole in that carpet—"

"I used the sledgehammer. She has been clearly told that my feelings for her are nonexistent. But you're the one I need to believe me, Regan. I'm not on the rebound from her—I never was. You figured it out long before I did. I didn't love her. She fit some textbook ideal of what I thought love was about. I never felt for her the way a man should love a woman. Can love a woman."

"Alex..." Whatever she started to say, she fell silent when he pivoted around to face her.

"The truth is—I didn't know the difference until I met you. Everything about you scared me from the first day. It definitely wasn't love at first sight. It was more terror at first sight. I wanted you like I'd die if I couldn't have you...couldn't eat, couldn't sleep for thinking about you. But I couldn't imagine your feeling the same, Regan. I was afraid of not being enough lover for you. I was afraid of becoming another on that long list of men who'd let you down. I wanted to be one of those legendary knights you were so afraid to believe in—only there was just no chance I could be more than a man."

"Dammit, Brennan, you're going to make me cry." She charged off the bed and hurled herself in his arms. "You're ten times any man I ever knew. I was the one who was scared. I was afraid you wanted a princess. A pastel damsel type...or at least somebody with a little elegance and dignity. I didn't see how I could ever fit in your life, not long-term."

"No one, ever, fit in my life like you do." He kissed her temple. Her nose. Her cheek. "That was part of the wonder of falling in love with you. Nothing went right for us. Nothing was *ideal*. From fumbling in the front seat of a car to my ex-fiancée showing up this morning to anything, everything. We met at the worst of times, with problems at every turn in the road. But we came together because of those problems. I kept discovering I could be honest with you, real with you, myself with you. I never felt that kind of freedom with anyone else."

"I never felt this kind of love," she whispered.

He kissed her mouth, not a taking but a giving. A wooing kiss, flavored with tenderness, warmed with all the promises for the future he felt in his heart. He took his time. Maybe anxiety had been tearing through his nerves for hours now, but her responsiveness assured him that he had all the time he needed. His Regan had always been so positive she responded only to chemistry. It was never so. Nothing made her respond as helplessly, as volatilely, as unforgettably...as love.

Eventually he lifted his head, stroked her cheek. "You know what I want to ask you," he murmured.

"I think so." Her face was tilted to his, her skin stroked with sunlight.

"I know you think we're different, love, but what I've seen from the start is that we believe in exactly the same things. Honor, commitment, loyalty, chivalry. Now, don't give me an argument on that word *chivalry*, Ms. Stuart, because I already know you're an unshakably militant feminist. But you believe in protecting those you love, no differently than I do. You rescued me. That's the truth. I might have been lonely my whole life if you hadn't.''

''That goes both ways, Alex. You rescued me right back. I really didn't believe in magic...not until I met you and discovered how real the magic of love can be.''

He smiled. That same delicious, wicked smile that put an ooga booga in her pulse the first time she'd met him. Then he said, ''I'm thinking we need a bunch of children running around this giant house. I'll teach the girls to be miniature militant feminists. You can teach the boys the legendary heroic values. Somehow I can already picture big, noisy arguments over dishes. But I know it'll work, if we start out by showing them love. Real love. Enduring love. You have any corrections you want to make in that program so far?''

She shook her head, her eyes glistening like diamonds.

His smile faded, and his face turned grave. ''I love you, more than my own heart,'' he said softly. ''Would you wear my ring and bear my name, Regan? Live with me, learn with me, love with me. Be my lifelong bride?''

''Yes.'' She wrapped her arms tightly around him. ''Oh, yes.'' She pelted his face with kisses, each a confession, each a vow. She understood his fears, because love had exposed her most terrifying fears the same way...and her most vulnerable dreams. Her mate, her lover, needed some confidence building. It was a perfect job for a woman who loved him.

And Regan had never been looking for some ideal ''right man.'' She'd been searching for a man to love her...the right way. Alex knew her, like no one else. He knew her fears; he knew her flaws; there had never been a chance or a reason to pretend with him. He loved the woman she was and could become…

With him.

* * * * * *

FANTASTIC NEWS!

For all you devoted Diana Palmer fans
Silhouette Books is pleased to bring you
a brand-new novel and short story by one of the
top ten romance writers in America

"Nobody tops Diana Palmer...I love her stories."
—New York Times **bestselling author
Jayne Ann Krentz**

**Diana Palmer has written another thrilling desire.
Man of the Month Ramon Cortero was a talented
surgeon, existing only for his work—until the
night he saved nurse Noreen Kensington's life. But
their stormy past makes this romance a challenge!**

THE PATIENT NURSE
Silhouette Desire
October 1997

And in November Diana Palmer adds to the
Long, Tall Texans series with *CHRISTMAS COWBOY*, in
LONE STAR CHRISTMAS, a fabulous new holiday
keepsake collection by talented authors Diana Palmer
and Joan Johnston. Their heroes are seductive,
shameless and irresistible—and these Texans are
experts at sneaking kisses under the mistletoe! So get
ready for a sizzling holiday season....

Only from **V**™ *Silhouette*®

Take 4 bestselling love stories FREE

Plus get a FREE surprise gift!

Special Limited-time Offer

Mail to Silhouette Reader Service™

3010 Walden Avenue
P.O. Box 1867
Buffalo, N.Y. 14240-1867

YES! Please send me 4 free Silhouette Desire® novels and my free surprise gift. Then send me 6 brand-new novels every month, which I will receive months before they appear in bookstores. Bill me at the low price of $2.90 each plus 25¢ delivery and applicable sales tax, if any.* That's the complete price and a savings of over 10% off the cover prices—quite a bargain! I understand that accepting the books and gift places me under no obligation ever to buy any books. I can always return a shipment and cancel at any time. Even if I never buy another book from Silhouette, the 4 free books and the surprise gift are mine to keep forever.

225 BPA A3UU

Name	(PLEASE PRINT)	
Address	Apt. No.	
City	State	Zip

This offer is limited to one order per household and not valid to present Silhouette Desire® subscribers. *Terms and prices are subject to change without notice.
Sales tax applicable in N.Y.

UDES-696

ATTENTION
ALL JOAN JOHNSTON FANS!

Silhouette Books is pleased to bring you two brand-new additions to the #1 bestselling Hawk's Way series—the novel you've all been waiting for and a short story....

"Joan Johnston does contemporary westerns to perfection." —*Publishers Weekly*

Remember those Whitelaws of Texas from Joan Johnston's HAWK'S WAY series? Jewel Whitelaw is all grown up and is about to introduce Mac Macready to the wonders of passion! You see, Mac is a virgin...and it's going to be one long, hot summer....

HAWK'S WAY
THE VIRGIN GROOM
August 1997

And in November don't miss Rolleen Whitelaw's love story, *A HAWK'S WAY CHRISTMAS*, in **LONE STAR CHRISTMAS**, a fabulous new holiday keepsake collection by talented authors Joan Johnston and Diana Palmer. Their heroes are seductive, shameless and irresistible—and these Texans are experts in sneaking kisses under the mistletoe! So get ready for a sizzling holiday season....

Only from ▼ *Silhouette*®

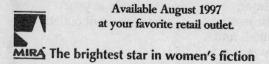

They called her the

Champagne Girl

Catherine: Underneath the effervescent, carefree and bubbly facade there was a depth to which few had access.

Matt: The older stepbrother she inherited with her mother's second marriage, Matt continually complicated things. It seemed to Catherine that she would make plans only to have Matt foul them up.

With the perfect job waiting in New York City, only one thing would be able to keep her on a dusty cattle ranch: something she thought she could never have—the love of the sexiest cowboy in the Lone Star state.

by bestselling author

DIANA PALMER

Available in September 1997 at your favorite retail outlet.

MIRA The brightest star in women's fiction   MDP8

Look us up on-line at: http://www.romance.net

SILHOUETTE®

Desire®

EXTRA***EXTRA***EXTRA
Temptation, Texas, advertises for women.

Salt-of-the-earth bachelors in search of
Mrs. Happily-ever-after. Read what the men of the
town have to say about their search:

Harley Kerr: I've lived my whole life in Temptation, Texas,
and I don't know what this foolish business about needing
women is all about. I've already done the wedded-bliss thing
once, and I'd rather wrestle a Texas rattler than walk down
the aisle again! **(MARRY ME, COWBOY, SD#1084, 7/97)**

Hank Braden: Women! I love 'em! The shape of 'em, the feel
of 'em, the scent of 'em. But I don't expect to be getting
permanently attached to any of them! I've got too many wild
oats to sow to be contemplating marriage!
(A LITTLE TEXAS TWO-STEP, SD#1090, 8/97)

Cody Fipes: When I suggested advertising for women, it
wasn't for *me!* There's only ever been one woman for me....
Besides, with all these new folks moving into Temptation,
I've got too much to do as sheriff to spend time investigating
a wife! **(LONE STAR KIND OF MAN, SD#1096, 9/97)**

**Starting in July from Silhouette Desire and Peggy Moreland,
three tales about love—and trouble—in Texas!**

**TROUBLE IN TEXAS.... When Temptation beckons,
three rugged cowboys lose their hearts.**

Available wherever Silhouette books are sold.